Hedgerow Tales

Suddenly there came a dark shape from the shadow of the hedgerow and the terrified newt, glancing upwards, caught sight of sharp bared teeth.

'Rat!' he cried, slipping under a stone. 'Rat! Beware!'

One of the lizards, the smaller one, slipped under the stone with him, trembling with fright. But where was the big lizard?

Other Enid Blyton Titles published by Red Fox:

Naughty Amelia Jane
Amelia Jane Again
The Hidey Hole
Snowball the Pony
The Adventurous Four
The Adventurous Four Again
The Children of Cherry Tree Farm
The Children of Willow Farm
Josie Click and Bun Stories
Mr Meddle Stories
Mr Pinkwhistle Stories
Mr Twiddle Stories
The Naughtiest Girl in the School
The Naughtiest Girl is a Monitor
Circus Days Again
Come to the Circus
Hurrah for the Circus
Mr Galliano's Circus
The Six Bad Boys
Buttercup Farm Family
The Caravan Family
The Pole Star Family
The Queen Elizabeth Family
Saucy Jane Family
The Seaside Family
The Goblin Aeroplane and Other Stories
The Little Green Imp and Other Stories
The Birthday Kitten and The Boy Who Wanted a Dog

HEDGEROW TALES

by

Enid Blyton

Illustrated by
Sarah Silcock

RED FOX

A Red Fox Book
Published by Arrow Books Limited
20 Vauxhall Bridge Road, London SW1V 2SA
An imprint of the Random Century Group
London Melbourne Sydney Auckland
Johannesburg and agencies throughout the world

These stories were first published in *Hedgerow Tales* by Methuen
Children's Books in 1935
Red Fox edition 1990
Text © Darrell Waters Ltd 1935

Phototypeset in Plantin
by Input Typesetting Ltd, London

Made and printed in Great Britain by
Courier International Ltd, Tiptree, Essex

ISBN 0 09 973580 6

Contents

Rabbity Ways

The night had been very dark, for there was no moon. Now there was a grey light creeping into the eastern sky. Daybreak was near. Soon the owls would go home and the bats would fly back to the old barn to sleep.

The old oak-tree that grew out of the hedge-row rustled its leaves in the chilly wind. It was a wise old tree, friendly to all creatures, and loved by a great many.

The hedgerow was old, too. In it grew haw-thorn, whose leaves were out early in the spring-time, green fingers held up to the sun. Bramble sprays flung long arms here and there, as prickly as the wild rose that forced its way up to the sun. Ivy covered one part of the hedge, and here, in blossom-time, feasted the last late flies and many beautiful red admirals.

Below was a sunny bank, for the hedgerow faced south. In summer-time the birds found sweet wild strawberries on this bank, and the primroses sometimes flowered there in the early days of January. In the ditch below there was moss growing, soft as velvet, and a few graceful ferns. It was always damp there and cool.

Near the old oak-tree was a small pond, ringed round with rushes and meadow-sweet. Many creatures came to drink there – from the sly red fox down to the striped yellow wasp! All the creatures in the fields around knew the pond well, and often the swallows would come and skim above it, looking for flies.

The hedgerow was in a deserted corner of the field. Nobody came there, not even the children hunting for blackberries. The farmer had forgotten to cut the hedge for years, and it had grown tall and tangled. Sometimes the wind would bring the sound of the farmer's voice, shouting in a distant field to his horses, but usually the hedgerow knew nothing but the sound of the wind, of bird calls, and pattering paws.

Many, many things had happened in and around the hedgerow. The oak-tree had rustled its leaves over thousands of insects, birds and animals. Its twigs knew the difference between a squirrel's scampering paws and a bird's light hold, three toes in front and one behind. Its acorns had been stolen by all kinds of mice, and by the screeching jays and the hungry nut-hatch.

Now it stood whispering in the cool wind of daybreak. Summer was passing over, and soon the oak-leaves would lose their dark green hue and would turn brown.

The grey light in the sky became brighter. Beneath the oak-tree, where the bank showed a sandy streak, a hole could just be seen. It was a rabbit's burrow. The burrow went down among the roots of the tree, exactly the size of a rabbit's body except now and again when it widened out to make passing-places for two meeting rabbits. The tunnel branched off into two or three different burrows, but the rabbits had learnt every foot of them, and always knew which tunnel to take when they wanted to go to the gorse-bush, to the bank or to the other side of the pond.

Out of the hole in the bank a rabbit's head appeared. Her big eyes looked through the dim grey light, her nose twitched as she sniffed the air, and her big ears listened to every sound. She wanted to go out and feed on the grass, and she had with her a young family of five rabbits, who were just getting old enough to look after themselves.

'It is safe,' she said to her young ones. 'We can go out. There is no stoat about, and the owls have all gone home.'

They trooped out of the hole. Other rabbits were in the field too, big ones and little ones, for there were many other burrows there.

'Keep near the burrow,' said the mother rabbit. 'Then you will not have far to run if danger comes. I am going along the hedgerow. There is a young furze-bush there and I shall feed on the juicy shoots. Keep an eye on the other rabbits, and if you see them turn so that their white bobtail shows plainly, dart into your burrow. Bobbing tails mean danger somewhere! And keep your ears pricked, too – for

11

if one of the old rabbits scents danger he will drum on the ground with his hind foot to warn us all. Then you must run as fast as you can.'

The little rabbits began to nibble the grass. They felt quite sure they could look after themselves. Their mother ran silently along the hedgerow. Suddenly she stopped and stood so still that it seemed as if she had frozen stiff. She had seen another animal coming through the hedge.

It was a brown hare. As soon as the rabbit saw that it was a harmless creature she ran on again and came up to the hare.

'You scared me, cousin hare,' she said. 'Is your burrow round here?'

'Burrow!' said the hare, looking in surprise at the rabbit, her soft eyes gleaming in the grey light. 'I have no burrow. I live above ground.'

'But how dangerous!' said the rabbit in alarm. 'Stoats and weasels could easily find you! Do you make a nest like the birds?'

'Come with me,' said the hare. 'I will show you where I live. My home is called a form, because it is simply a dent in the ground the size and form of my body. I make it the shape of my body by lying in it, you see. I like to live alone. I should not like to live with others, as you do.'

'But it is safer,' said the rabbit, going with the hare over the field. 'I have left my young ones with the other rabbits, and they will warn them if danger is near. There is safety in numbers.'

'My ears and my nose make me safe,' said the hare. 'I can smell far-away things and hear the slightest noise. Look at my ears, longer than yours, cousin. See the black tips, too. You have no black tips. Look at my hind legs. Yours are strong, but mine are much stronger. I can run like the wind!'

Suddenly the hare gave a great leap, and jumped about fifteen feet over the field. The rabbit was startled but the hare called to her.

'Here is my form. I always jump like that before I go to it, so that I break my trail. Then if weasel or stoat come round they cannot follow my scent, for it breaks where I jump! Come here, cousin. I have some young ones to show you, only a few days old.'

The rabbit went to the hare's form, which was simply a dent in the earth. Near it were other small holes, and in each lay a young hare, a leveret, its eyes wide open, its body warmly covered with fur.

'They have made forms of their own,' said

the hare, proudly. 'Even when they are young they like to live alone.'

'My young ones were not like this,' said the rabbit in surprise, looking at the leverets. 'My children were born blind and deaf and had no fur on them at all. I made a special burrow for them, and blocked up the entrance to it every time I went out. I should not think of leaving them out in the open like this. It is a good thing your children are born able to see and hear, or they would certainly be eaten by an enemy!'

'They are safe enough,' said the hare. 'Now take me to see your home, cousin rabbit. I should like to see your youngsters, too.'

They went back to the hedgerow. The hare gave another great leap when she left her form. It was a favourite trick of hers not only when leaving her home, but when she was hunted by dogs. Sometimes she would double on her tracks, too, to throw off her hunters. It nearly always deceived them.

The hare was astonished to see the burrow in which the rabbits lived. 'But how do you manage about your ears?' she asked. 'Do you bend them back when you run underground? That must be very uncomfortable. It is a strange idea to tunnel in the earth. I am sure that our family were not meant to do so, or we would not have been given such long ears. It must be difficult, too, to dig out all the earth.'

'No, it is easy,' said the rabbit. 'I dig with my front paws and shovel out the earth with my hind paws. See, cousin, there are my children feeding.'

The hare was looking at the young rabbits in the light of the dawn when a curious noise came to her long ears. It was a drumming sound, and it seemed to the hare as if the ground were quivering under her feet. The mother rabbit called to her young ones at once.

'Come here! There is danger about! That is the old rabbit drumming with his hind feet to warn us. Come, cousin, you must hide in our burrow, too.'

The young rabbits lifted their heads when they heard the drumming. Then they saw all the other rabbits running in every direction to their holes, their white bobtails showing clearly. The young ones were off, too, and scampered to their hole. Not a rabbit was to be seen when the old red fox came slinking by.

The hare had gone, too – but not down the burrow.

'My legs are safer than a burrow!' she thought to herself. 'I shall run, not hide! No fox can catch *me*!'

'Poor hare!' thought the rabbit. 'She ought to dig a burrow, then she would be safe. The fox will surely get her.'

But the fox went hungry that morning!

Prickly Friends

There were many holes in the bank under the hedgerow. Some were big, some were small, but nearly all of them had some creature living there. A hole made a safe and warm hiding-place, a home to come back to after wanderings in the fields. The leaves of the oak-tree knew all the holes, for they drifted there when they fell, or were taken into them by the little creatures who wanted to line the holes for winter nests.

There was one very nice hole, tucked under a jutting-out piece of bank so that it could hardly be seen. It did not look very big from the outside, because a curtain of moss hung over the entrance. But inside it was very roomy. It had been dug out the summer before by a colony of wasps. The queen wasp had started the hole, and when her first eggs had hatched into grubs and then into wasps her children had helped her to make the hole bigger and bigger to hold the growing nest.

17

But one night the big badger had come prowling by and had smelt out the wasps. He liked the taste of the fat wasp grubs, so he put his big clawed foot into the hole and scraped until he had the nest out. It was a grey, papery thing, full of eggs, grubs and live wasps. They were frightened of this attack in the dark, and although they tried hard to sting the badger they could not pierce his thick hide.

He ate all the eggs and grubs and destroyed so many of the wasps that the nest was not rebuilt again and the hole was deserted. A mouse went in and finished up what was left of the nest, and when the autumn came the wind blew in a great heap of oak-leaves. The little mouse used the hole as a larder, and stored there a hazelnut and two acorns.

He was there one day in summer, when he heard a snuffling and shuffling in the damp ditch below. Then a pig-like snout was suddenly pushed into the hole and the mouse sat frozen with fright. It was a hedgehog! Now a hedgehog thinks nothing of making a meal of a small brown mouse, and the tiny creature thought his last moment had come. But the hedgehog was very full of worms and slugs, and she had no room for a mouse just then. So when she withdrew her snout from the hole the

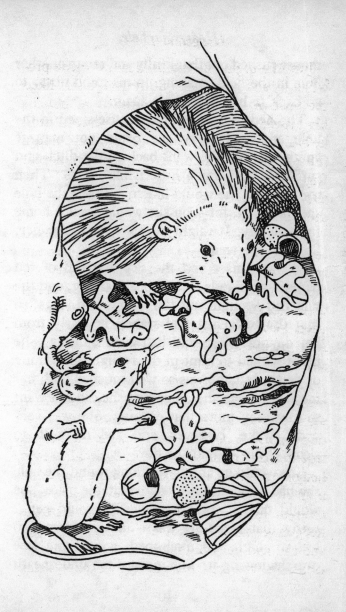

mouse rushed out thankfully and ran to another hole in the field, making up his mind never to go back to his larder-hole again.

The hedgehog smelt the mouse-smell in the hole and was sorry she could not manage another meal. She went back to the ditch and snuffled about for a little while longer. Then she felt that she would like to examine the hole she had seen, for soon she would want a home for a family. It might be big enough for her. So back she went.

It was sunset and the sky was full of red banked-up clouds. It had been raining, and the rain had brought out the worms and slugs, so that the hedgehog had waked up early from her daytime sleep and had gone hunting. She usually liked to hunt in the twilight of evening or dawn, but she was so well satisfied with her meal of worms and slugs that she did not want to hunt any more that evening. She was very wide awake, however, and had no wish to sleep. What should she do?

She would go and have a look round the hole she had seen, and if it was a suitable place, she would take it for her own. She could get it ready that night. It was a nice hedgerow to live in, high and unclipped, with a big tree overshadowing it. The moist ditch underneath was a fine place for hunting, and the pond near by would give her water to drink. She went back to the hole.

The mouse was gone, of course. The hedgehog pushed her way in. It was a tight fit at the entrance, but inside the hole was quite roomy. There were dead oak-leaves there, dry and brittle, from last autumn, and two acorn shells and a gnawed hazel-nut. The hedgehog turned round and round in the hole, and then lay down with her snout pointing towards the entrance, so that she could see if anyone came by. The moss hung down a little to hide it, but she could quite well see the evening light outside, filtering into the hole. It was a good hole.

'It shall be mine,' thought the hedgehog. 'Here I will bring up my children, for there will be plenty of food in the ditch for them. They will be safe here.'

When the little mouse ventured near to the hole one day in August he heard a strange noise coming from it – a hoarse sound that came and went as he listened. Whatever could it be?

He crept nearer, and was at last bold enough to push aside the mossy curtain and look in. One peep was enough! He fled down the bank and threw himself into the tall stinging-nettles. The hedgehog was there – fast asleep and snoring, it is true, but with her were wide-awake children, their beady eyes sharply watching the entrance of their home!

'The hole I used for my winter-larder is taken by a hedgehog and her family,' the little mouse told the rabbit that lived down the burrow under the oak-tree. 'Go and see.'

The rabbit was interested to hear of the new-comers, and she watched to see who came from the hole in the bank. She had not long to wait, for one fine September night, just when it was dusk and the moon was rising, the hedgehog put her snout out of the hole and after she had snuffed the air, came out quickly. Behind her came seven curious little creatures, with short grey spines – her children.

The hedgehog saw the watching rabbit at once, but did not fear her. She set about hunt-ing for food, and very soon crunched up a few beetles, one worm, a big snail, and a small green frog. The little hedgehogs ran about like clockwork, their short legs twinkling under-neath them. They rooted out beetles, and were pleased to find slugs eating a toadstool.

'Keep near me,' called their mother, warn-ingly. 'The badger may be about, or the fox, and remember you cannot roll up into a ball yet as I can. You will not be able to until you are a year old, so be careful until then.'

'How do you roll up?' asked the rabbit, looking at the hedgehog's prickly body. 'Show me.'

At once the hedgehog curled herself up so tightly that she looked exactly like a round ball of prickles. Her head was hidden, and she lay as still as stone. Soon she unrolled herself and looked proudly at the rabbit.

'I am well armoured!' she said. 'I am afraid of few enemies – the badger, perhaps, and the fox.'

'But surely the fox can't eat you,' said the rabbit, trembling a little at the mention of her cunning enemy. 'Your prickles would make his mouth bleed.'

'He can only get me if I unroll myself,' said the hedgehog, 'and he makes me uncurl by a very horrible trick. He is an evil-smelling creature when he likes, and as I cannot bear him at his smelliest, I uncurl to get away. Then he can catch me easily. But my short, sharp prickles make all other creatures drop me in a hurry if they try to eat me!'

'I wish I had your spines!' said the rabbit, longingly. 'But I only have my strong, swift legs to help me when enemies are near.'

Suddenly there came the sound of a pitiful

wail through the dusk. The hedgehog scuttled towards it at once, for she knew the cry of her young ones. The rabbit bolted headlong into her hole, and all the rabbits near by did the same.

'Badger! Badger!' murmured all the creatures of the hedgerow, lying low with their ears well pricked and their eyes bright. 'Badger! He has come down from the hills.'

The hedgehog met her young ones hurrying towards her – but one was gone.

'A great creature suddenly came upon us,' said the young hedgehogs, shaking with fear. 'He had heavy clawed feet, and his muzzle was pointed. He ate one of us. Let us go to our hole before he comes after us.'

The mother hedgehog pushed her children before her and they ran to the hedgerow as fast as they could on their short feet. All their prickles bristled as they ran, though the spines of the young ones were soft compared with their mother's. They clambered up the bank and one by one squeezed into the hole, the mother following last of all. The small hedgehogs cuddled close to her, although she was not a comfortable mother to love. There they all lay, their hearts beating fast, remembering the little hedgehog who cried so pitifully as the badger caught him.

One little hedgehog began to squeak with fright as he remembered.

'Hush,' warned the mother. 'The badger may come this way. Listen! You can hear the thud of his heavy tread.'

They all listened, snug in their hole, the night sky outside lit up by the silver moon. The badger was looking for another meal, for he was hungry. He decided to hunt for mice and came along the ditch, his heavy feet scuffling the leaves as he walked. The hedgehogs lay breathless in their hole. If the badger smelt them out, it would not be long before all the young ones, at least, were eaten.

There were no mice to be found. The badger raised his snout in the air and sniffed. He thought he smelt a faint scent of hedgehog. Then a sound startled him and he lumbered off over the field, away from the hedgerow. He was gone.

'Come out,' said the rabbit, appearing at the hedgehog's hole. 'The moon is in the sky, and the badger has gone. There is good hunting for you tonight.'

But the hedgehogs did not stir abroad that night. The next night they left their hole to find another, for they were afraid that the badger might come back.

'Goodbye,' said the hedgehog to the rabbit. 'I shall see you again, for when winter comes and I want to sleep, I shall come back to that good hole, I think. It is so warm and comfortable, and if I line it with leaves and moss it will make a fine sleeping-place. Goodbye till then!'

Then away she went with her six prickly children, little grey shadows in the moonlight.

New Tails for Old

The little pond that lay quietly by the old hedgerow had a few yellow leaves on its surface one early October morning. Autumn was coming, and the mornings and evenings were chilly. The water in the pond was not so warm now as it had been in the summer, and September's rain had filled it well, so that it was quite deep in the middle.

There was a warm, sandy patch on the bank near the pond, and on this sunny spot two small lizards liked to lie. They had lived there for a long time, for the hedgerow was undisturbed by humans, and not many of their enemies came along in the daytime. In the pond below lived a friend of theirs, a smooth newt, a creature very like themselves in shape; they often talked to him and heard the pond news, and in return told him the news of the hedgerow.

They had seen him in the water one day, swimming to and fro. As they watched him they saw him rubbing his mouth and nose as if something hurt him there. He used his small front feet like hands, and it seemed to the watching lizards as if he were trying to undo the skin round his mouth. It was ragged there, and looked as if it were peeling off.

Suddenly all the skin on the newt's head became loose and at once the little creature began to wriggle about violently. Then the skin on his back loosened. It was a strange thing to see. The newt tried to take his feet out of the loose skin, but he could not. So he climbed out of the water and rubbed himself against a stone to loosen the skin. It was then that he saw the watching lizards, their eyelids blinking every now and again. For a moment the newt looked as if he were going to plunge back into the pond, but one of the lizards, the bigger one of the two, spoke to him.

'You are casting your skin,' he said. 'We do that, too, but only in patches, not our whole skin at once as you are doing. Rub harder against the stone, newt – your skin will soon peel off altogether.'

The newt rubbed himself hard, and to his delight the skin became so loose that he was able to take his front legs out of their old skin covering. He slid down into the pond, wriggled

again and at last swam right out of his old skin,
leaving it floating in the water behind him, like
a little ghost of himself. He felt better then,
and once more climbed out upon the ,sunny
bank to talk to the little lizards.

That was the beginning of their friendship.
The lizards were bigger than the four-inch-long
newt, and their skins were different, for their
bodies were covered with small scales, like
those on the bodies of snakes. The newt had a
smooth skin, like a frog. He was olive brown
on his back, but underneath he was a pretty
orange colour, spotted with black. He proudly
showed the lizards his lovely orange under-
surface, but they at once raised themselves up
and showed him that they, too, had a glowing
orange colour on their underside.

'We are alike in many things,' said the lizards. 'We should be friends. Tell us, newt,
why do you like the water so much? *We* would
not swim in it no matter how warm it was.'

'Well, I was born in the water,' said the
newt. 'I was one of five or six eggs laid against
the leaf of a water-plant. My mother folded the
leaf over so that the eggs could not be seen. I
hatched out into a tadpole.'

'A tadpole!' said the bigger lizard. 'But tadpoles grow into frogs!'

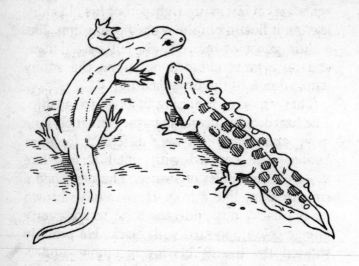

'Not always,' said the newt. 'Sometimes they grow into toads, and sometimes, if the eggs are laid by a newt, they grow into newts! I grew into a long, fish-like tadpole. I expect you must have seen me swimming about in the pond when I was as small as that. But when the frog tadpoles lost their tails, I kept mine, because it is so useful in swimming.'

'Ah,' said the smaller lizard. 'You were wise to keep your tail. Tails are useful things. You never know what help your tail will be to you.'

'But what help is *your* tail?' asked the newt in surprise.

'Sh!' said one of the lizards, quickly, as a buzzing noise was heard. 'Don't move. There are some bluebottle flies coming. They make a very tasty meal.'

All three were quiet, and soon four large bluebottles flew down and settled on the warm bank. With one swift movement the two lizards and the newt caught a bluebottle each, and the fourth fly shot away in panic.

'Very nice,' said the newt, swallowing. 'All kinds of flies are good.'

'And slugs, too, and spiders,' said the bigger lizard. 'I remember once catching a –'

But what he was going to say the newt never knew, for suddenly there came a dark shape from the shadow of the hedgerow, and the terrified newt, glancing upwards, caught sight of sharp bared teeth.

'Rat!' he cried, slipping under a stone. 'Rat! Beware!'

One of the lizards, the smaller one, slipped under the stone with him, trembling with fright. But where was the big lizard? The two under the stone peeped out in fear, wondering if their companion had been eaten.

They saw a strange sight. The rat had pounced on the big lizard and had got him by the tapering tail. But, even as the two watchers looked on in horror, they saw the tail break off neatly, just as if were made of brittle glass – and the lizard, tailless but safe, glided to cover in a thick clump of grass. The rat made as if he would go after the escaping lizard, but he could not help watching the strange behaviour of the tail. It was jumping about as if it were alive! The rat at once put his paw on it, and forgot all about the lizard. In a second he had eaten the wriggling tail, and then ran off into the hedgerow.

After a long while the lizard and the newt crept out once more into the sunshine – and to their joy they were joined by the other lizard too, looking rather queer and short because of his lost tail.

'It will grow again!' he said to the newt. 'That is just a good lizard trick. If an enemy catches me, I break off my tail, and leave it jumping about to attract his attention whilst I safely escape. I shan't have such a *nice* tail for my second one, but still, I'm alive, and that's all I care about. Didn't I tell you that tails were useful, newt?'

'You did,' said the newt. 'Well, I hope mine will be as useful to *me*! Now I am going back to the pond for a swim, so goodbye.'

All this had happened in the summer-time

and now it was autumn. The lizards were finding the mornings very cold, and they came out
later and later. They had a very cosy hole under
a big stone, and here they had decided to sleep
for the winter, when they could find no flies to
eat, and were too cold to go hunting for spiders.

'I wish the newt would come and join us,'
said the big lizard, blinking his eyelids sleepily
in the October sunshine. 'We should sleep well
together, the three of us, all our tails curled
round one another.'

'Your new tail has grown well,' said the
smaller lizard. 'It isn't so long as the other, but
it does quite well. Look! There is the newt
swimming just below us in the pond. Call him.'

But before the lizards could do anything to
attract the newt's attention there came the loud
flap-flap-flap of large wings, and a great heron
flew slowly down to the pond. It stood on its
long legs not far from the lizards, who at once
fled under their stone. Then the big bird put
its head on one side and watched for a fish or
a frog, for it was hungry on this cold October
morning.

The newt had been busy eating a water-grub
and had not noticed the heron. All he saw now
was what looked like two great sticks of yellow
in the water – the legs of the waiting heron,

although the newt did not know it. The little
creature swam about below, little guessing that
the big heron, with its long strong beak, was
watching his every movement out of sharp and
hungry eyes. Suddenly the heron flashed its
long beak into the water, trying to spear the
newt – but just in time the frightened animal
darted off – only to find that the heron, instead
of stabbing him through the body, had got him
by the tail!

He wriggled desperately as the heron lifted
up his head to take him from the water and
swallow him whole – and then he remembered
how the lizard had escaped from the rat by

breaking off his tail. Quickly the newt did the same, dropping back safely into the water, leaving his poor little tail in the beak of the disappointed heron. He was saved – but how queer it was to swim through the water without a tail! He could not get along.

He hid under a stone in the water until the heron had flown off. Then awkwardly he clambered up the bank to where his two lizard friends awaited him.

'Tails *are* useful,' he told them. 'I hope mine will grow in time for the spring. But now it is autumn and if you will have me, I will hide with you under your stone to sleep for the winter-time.'

Then all three curled up close together, their little feet holding tightly to one another, and there they sleep soundly in the safety of their stone-shelter under the old hedgerow. Not even the rat guesses where they are.

The Adventurers

October days had been sunny and warm, and there were many blackberries ripe in the hedgerow. Some of the bramble-leaves were turning scarlet and gold, and glowed brightly when the sun shone through them. The ivy was blooming on the hedge just below the oak-tree, and to it came hundreds of bluebottle flies, late butterflies, wasps, bees and little creeping insects. It was the last feast of the year before winter set in.

The swallows and the martins had revelled in the warm October sunshine, but they did not like the chilly nights. The oak-tree felt the wind of their wings all day long as they flew round, for many of the insects that fed on the ivy-flowers below flew up into the air when they were satisfied, and were chased and caught by the keen-eyed swallows. The martins, too, knew where the ivy blossom was, with its insects, and darted up and down over the hedge, catching unwary bluebottles as they buzzed noisily over the ivy.

The rabbits, peeping out of their holes, knew the birds well. They had arrived one April morning, when the south wind was blowing strongly, a great crowd of them together, crying, 'Feetafeetit, feetafeetit' to one another. They were weary little birds then, but very happy. They had flown a long way to come to the fields they knew, for they all wished to nest in the spot they had loved so well the year before.

'There is the oak-tree!' they cried to one another as they circled round it. 'And see, here is the hedgerow where the ivy blooms later on! We are home again!'

Then off they flew to find the old barn where each year the swallows built their nests, and the old farmhouse against which the house-martins liked to put their homes of mud. It was lovely to be home again after being away all the long winter. Now sunny days, clouds of insects to eat, the joys of nesting and bringing up young ones lay before them, and the little birds were happy.

The creatures of the hedgerow did not very often speak to the flying swallows and martins, because, unlike other birds, they seldom perched on trees or bushes. All day long they flew in the air, and the rabbits grew used to their musical voices, twittering from dawn to dusk.

When they were making their nests the two lizards who lived on the bank near the pond watched the pretty little birds in surprise – for both swallows and martins came down to the pond-side and scraped up mud in their beaks! The lizards thought at first that they were eating the mud, and wondered if there were insects in it.

'Why do you eat mud?' asked one lizard. 'It has no taste.'

The swallow could not answer because her beak was full of mud – but another swallow, who had just flown down to the pond-side, answered the lizard.

'We are not eating mud!' she said, with a twittering, laughing sound. 'We are taking it to build our nests.'

'But nests are not built of mud,' said the lizard, who had seen a robin building her nest in the hedgerow bank the year before, and thought he knew all about nests. 'They are built of roots, leaves and moss.'

'Not ours!' said the swallow. 'We make a saucer of mud on one of the beams of the old barn, and there we put our eggs, pretty white things with brown spots.'

38

'But doesn't the mud make your eggs dirty and wet?' asked the lizard.

'Of course not,' cried the swallow, thinking that the lizard must be very stupid. 'It dries hard and makes a fine nest. See, I will put a beakful of mud by your hole on the bank. You will see that it gets quite hard when it dries.'

The swallow dropped some mud in a tiny pile beside the lizard's hole and then went back to the pond-side again, scooping up some more mud in her beak. Then off she flew to the barn away across the field to dab the mud against the growing saucer-nest she was building.

The martins came to the pond as often as the swallows, and the lizards grew to know them well whilst they were nest-building. But as soon as the nests were finished the twittering birds came no more to the pond-side, but flew high in the blue summer sky all the day. Once or twice they saw the little lizards and called to them, but it was not until October came, with its chilly mornings and evenings, that the lizards saw the swallows to talk to once again.

Then they noticed that the telegraph wires that ran over the hedgerow, held up by a tall black pole, were quite weighted down with swallows and martins each evening. They seemed to be collecting together from all the

fields around. The lizards looked at them in wonder. They could see the swallows with their steel-blue backs, long forked tails and chestnut-coloured throats, and they knew that the other birds, with shorter tails and a white patch at the lower end of their backs, were the little house-martins.

Why were they all crowding together like this?

'Feetafeetit, feetafeetit!' cried the swallows, gaily. 'It is time to go!'

'Where to?' asked the lizards, calling out to a swallow that skimmed low over the pond, trying to catch a fly.

'To a warmer land!' said the swallow. 'Come with us!'

'How far is it?' asked the lizard.

'Hundreds, thousands of miles!' cried the swallow. 'We fly with the north wind. We must go!'

'But why must you go?' asked the lizard. 'Don't go, swallow! We like to hear your twittering.'

'We are going to a land where there are plenty of insects,' said the swallow. 'If we stay here for the cold days, we should die of hunger.'

'No, you wouldn't,' said the lizard. 'The robin stays, and the thrush and blackbird, and they feed on insects. *I* feed on insects, too.'

'Ah, but *you* go to sleep in the winter!' said the swallow. 'I know you do, because one spring we came back early and the lizards were still asleep in their holes, the lazy creatures! But we *must* go, lizard – I don't really know why we have to go, and I don't know the way – but when this time of year comes and the north wind begins to blow, something stirs inside me, and I feel I must fly to the south for miles upon miles!'

'It is a great adventure,' said the lizard.

'The greatest adventure in the world!' answered the swallow. 'We fly together in a big flock over the sea and over the land, over mountains and rivers, fields and forests. And all the time we cry to one another, for we are afraid of getting lost, especially at night or in a fog.'

'What if a storm comes?' asked the lizard, trembling as he remembered a great storm that had happened in the summer.

'Then we may perish!' said the swallow. 'But most of us get to the lands in the south, where the sun shines all day. We love it, but it isn't our home. We don't nest there. It is just a holiday for us, that's all! We shall all be longing for the spring to come again, for then one day we shall feel homesick for the fields and hills round here, and when the south wind blows to help us, we shall go with it – back to the old barns we love so well! I shall come back to my barn, and I will call to you as I dart over the hedgerow. Then you will know I have come back. You are sure you won't come with us?'

'How can I?' said the lizard, impatiently. 'I have no wings. Besides, I should be afraid. I am not used to adventuring as you are.'

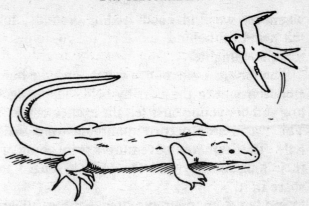

'Then goodbye!' called the swallow, and flew up to join his brothers and sisters on the telegraph wires. The lizard heard him excitedly twittering as he told all that had been said. The other birds twittered back, and the evening air was full of their sweet, high voices.

'Thank goodness they're going!' said a robin, suddenly, looking out of the hedgerow. 'They eat too many insects. Food will soon get scarce. I should drive away those swallows if they stayed round here!'

'Don't get in a temper!' cried the swallows, hearing his high, creamy trill. 'We are going tonight, tonight, tonight!'

'The north wind is blowing!' twittered the martins. 'The sky is clear. It is time to go. We need not fly all the way at once. We can rest whenever we find good feeding-grounds, for the wind is behind us. Let us go tonight, tonight, tonight!'

The rabbits came out to watch, and the hare stood upright in the near-by field. The hedge-hog and her young ones felt the excitement too. The two lizards peeped trembling from their hole. The feathered adventurers were going on their long journey! All the animals longed to share in it.

Suddenly, in their hundreds, the swallows flew into the evening air, circled round once or twice, and then, in a great cloud, flew towards the south. 'Feetafeetit, feetafeetit!' they called. 'Goodbye, goodbye! We will come back in the spring.'

They were gone. Soon not even the soft noise of their thousand wings could be heard. All the hedgerow creatures sighed and went back to their holes. They would miss the swallows and their bright voices – but the spring would bring them back again. Ah, but the spring was far away!

'What adventurers!' thought the rabbit, scuttling down her hole. 'What daring little adventurers!'

Oak-Tree Guests

The oak-tree that spread its branches over the hedgerow knew almost every bird of the countryside. It knew the starlings, who often sat in dozens among the leaves, chattering at the tops of their queer little voices. It knew the thrushes and the blackbirds, and heard them singing at dawn. The little red robins were its friends, and the noisy sparrows, with their cry of 'Philip, Philip!' It knew the feel of countless little feet, clinging closely to the twigs. It had felt the thrush wiping its beak after a feast on the berries in the hedge below. It had sheltered the close-hidden nests of all kinds of birds, and had been the first home of many youngsters.

The tree had heard the skylark singing in the early mornings, but it did not know the brown bird very well, for the lark liked to run on the ground, and seldom perched in a tree. Neither did the tree know the peewits, except for their wild cry, 'Poo-wee, poo-wee!' as they circled in their hundreds over the fields – for

the peewits never came to the oak-tree, prefer-
ring the open fields.

The oak had other friends besides birds. It
liked to feel the red squirrels scampering about
the branches, and it loved the touch of the
dormouse's tiny feet, when it ran up the trunk
to look for acorns. It was a wise old tree, always

beautiful, whatever the season of the year. In spring its leaves were pale green and tender; in summer it stood clothed in glossy dark green, and its shade was welcome to the creatures of the hedgerow; when autumn came it turned a pale russet brown, and all through the winter it stretched out strong bare branches to the sky, with a few brown leaves still rattling in the wind.

Now it was winter, and the branches were bare and cold. The wind whistled through them, and the birds no longer roosted there at night, but found a cosy place in the thick green ivy below. But in the daytime the oak-tree had many guests.

Some came for the acorns, a few of which still stood stiffly in their pipe-like holders on the twigs. Some came for the spiders and grubs that lay hidden in the crannies of the rough bark. The oak-tree was glad to see its guests, for many of the beetle-grubs were deadly enemies, and would kill the old tree with their boring, if the birds did not search for them and eat them.

One December day, when the wind blew cold, a sturdy slate-grey and chestnut bird flew over the hedgerow. It whistled cheerfully, like a schoolboy – 'Tui, tui, tui!' The oak-tree knew that call well, for it had heard it all through the spring. The nuthatch had nested in the tree then, and had brought up its young ones there.

There was a hole in the trunk of the oak-tree, and the nuthatch had put dead leaves and grass into it, making a cosy nest for the eggs. The hole had been rather too big, so the clever bird had brought clay and blocked up the entrance until it was the right size. One day another little bird had come and peeped in the hole – a small brown bird, silvery white underneath.

It was a tree-creeper, looking for a place for its nest. It pulled at a piece of loose bark and wondered if it should stuff moss and grass behind it for a nest. But then the nuthatch had come rushing out of its hole and frightened it away – so it had nested in another tree, behind an ivy-stem, not very far away.

Another day a spotted woodpecker had come, and with his strong beak had drummed on the bark of the oak-tree. The noise had disturbed the young nuthatches, and the mother bird came to the entrance of the nest-hole to see what was the matter.

'What are you doing?' she cried, shrilly. 'You cannot nest in this tree. It is ours!'

'I am looking for an old half-dead tree,' said

the woodpecker, drumming again on the bark. 'I don't like to build my nest in a healthy tree – it is so difficult to drill a hole in the wood for a nest. But it is easy to peck out dead wood, and make a hole deep down in the trunk.'

'This tree is no use to you,' said the nut-hatch, sharply. 'It is an old tree, but alive and strong. You will find no dead wood in it. Go away, you disturb us with your loud drumming. There is an old pine on the hill that was struck with lightning last autumn – a big branch of it is dead and you could easily drill a nest-hole there.'

The woodpecker flew off, and the nuthatch heard him drumming on the pine, although it was half a mile away. It was a fine place for a nest, and the woodpecker soon made a hole there. Five small woodpeckers hatched out of the creamy-white eggs, and were quite happy and comfortable on the wood chips that served them for a nest at the bottom of the hole.

Now all the youngsters of the woodpecker, the treecreeper and the nuthatch had flown away, and were seeking their fortunes in the countryside round about. The days had been cold and frosty and food was not easy to find. The old woodpecker was wily and knew the best trees for hunting – and that was how he remembered the oak-tree on this cold winter's day.

He flew off to it, his gay plumage showing up brightly in the winter sunshine. His wings were barred with black and white, he had bright patches of white on his shoulders, and gay splashes of crimson on the nape of his neck and under his body near his tail.

He came to the oak-tree and perched on the trunk, two toes in front and two behind so that he might climb easily. His stiff tail feathers helped to support him and his strong beak sounded the furrowed bark. 'R-r-r-r-r-r-r-r!' He drummed on the trunk loudly because he was excited and wanted every one to know where he was.

He began to look for insects and spiders in the crevices of the bark. The small ones he took out with his long sticky tongue, the large ones he found by tapping and loosening the bark. He worked upwards and to the right – and just as he was going to pass under a branch he met another bird, much smaller than himself, also looking for insects in the trunk! Each was frightened and flew to a branch above. They looked at one another.

The second bird was the little brown tree-creeper. He had a long curved beak and bright eyes. He spoke humbly to the woodpecker.

'May I look for food in your tree?' he asked. 'It is a good tree. There are plenty of cocoons under the bark, and I have found some grubs too.'

'It is not my tree,' said the woodpecker. 'I did not nest here. But I don't want to share with you, tree-creeper. Find somewhere else to feed.'

The tree-creeper's sharp eyes saw a curled-up woodlouse in a cranny. He inserted his long curved beak behind the bark and pulled out the insect. The woodpecker watched him angrily, and fluffed out his feathers in rage.

'Quet, quet, quet, quet!' he cried, and was just going to rush at the tree-creeper when he heard a loud whistle from the top of the tree. Both birds looked up. It was the nuthatch, just arrived to look for any remaining acorns, or maybe a hazel-nut or two from the hedge below.

'This is *my* tree!' cried the nuthatch, and whistled again. 'Tui, tui, tui! This is *my* tree! I had my nest here, and brought up my young ones in a fine hole in the trunk. This is *my* tree! Go away, woodpecker and tree-creeper.'

The birds below looked up at the nuthatch.

He was slate-grey above and chestnut below, and through his eyes ran a dark stripe. The woodpecker did not move, but the tree-creeper was frightened and slipped underneath a branch, hanging there head downwards.

'You and I eat different food,' said the woodpecker to the nuthatch. 'We can feast on the same tree without interfering with one another. See, nuthatch, there are two hazel-nuts in the ditch below, fallen from the hedge. Take them before the mice find them.'

The nuthatch cocked his head on one side and looked into the ditch. He saw the nuts and flew down. He picked one up in his beak and flew back to the oak-tree with it. The woodpecker watched to see what he would do. How could he eat such a hard, woody thing?

The nuthatch was clever. He found a place in the bark of the trunk where he could press in the hazel-nut so that it stayed there, tightly gripped by the ridges of the bark. Then he held firmly on to the trunk with his strong feet, and began to hammer at the nutshell with his long beak. 'Tap-tap-tap! Tap-tap-tap!' He hammered at the nut until the shell broke. Then he quickly pecked out the kernel inside and swallowed it. That was his way of dealing with nuts!

He spied an acorn hanging on the oak-tree. He pecked it off, crying, 'Tui, tui, tui! I tell you this is *my* tree! Get away!'

The tree-creeper cried out in fright, and the woodpecker drummed in excitement on the trunk. Two jays, flying over from the wood, heard all the excitement and swooped down to see what it was about. One of them snatched the acorn from the nuthatch, and the other screeched harshly, 'Kraak, kraak, kraak! There are some acorns left. Let us have them!'

Off flew the tree-creeper, the woodpecker and the nuthatch, terrified of the big, screaming birds. 'It's a pity we quarrelled!' whistled the nuthatch. 'There was enough food for all of us, really! Meet me there tomorrow. Tui, tui, tui!'

One Warm Winter's Day

The weather had been cold and frosty. The ground had been as hard as iron, and when the bitter wintry wind blew, the dead leaves in the ditch had made a dry, crackling sound as they flew here and there. It had been hard weather for all the creatures still awake – the rabbits and hares, the weasels and stoats, the birds in the trees, the mice and the voles. They were hungry and cold. Only the sleepers were happy.

The dormouse slept comfortably in his cosy hole. The lizard and the newt knew nothing of the winter as they slept under the shelter of a big stone. The hedgehog snored gently in the bank, and the bat still hung upside down in a near-by cave, fast asleep.

A small, mouse-like creature poked his nose out of a hole in the bank one winter's day. It was a little field-vole with a short tail. He was not a mouse, for his body was rounded instead of long, and his ears were very short. His muzzle was not pointed like a mouse's, but was blunt. He sniffed the air before he came out from his hole. He knew that weasels and stoats were about, fierce with hunger, and he wanted to make sure he was safe.

The sun shone down on to the hedgerow bank. It felt warm to the little vole. There was no frost that morning. The New Year had come in softly and the weather had changed. For a little while it would be warmer. The field-vole was glad. He had been hiding in his burrow underground for a few days. The last time he had ventured out he had nearly been caught by a hungry weasel. Now he wanted a breath of fresh air and a word with his friends. Also he was thirsty, and he thought it would be safe to go to the pond for a drink.

He crept out of his hole. He was a dumpy little thing, and his tail really looked far too short for him. He sat for a minute in the sun. It was about noon, and the bank felt warm and comfortable. Then he scampered through the lank, straggling grasses of the bank and went to the edge of the little pond nearby. He was careful to keep under the grass as he went, and he did not move even a blade as he ran!

He was drinking from the pond when he heard a movement behind him, and he turned to run at once.

'Stay where you are,' said a squeaky voice. 'I shan't hurt you!'

The field-vole saw a creature about twice as big as he was, with a longer tail. He thought it was a brown rat, one of the many that lived about the pond and hunted fiercely all the year round. He was too frightened to move, and he crouched by the water, staring in fear at the creature just above him.

'Do you take me for a rat?' said the water-vole, amused. 'Indeed, I am nothing to do with the rats! I am a vole, like yourself, but as I can swim and dive well my name is *water*-vole. Look at me well and you will see I am your big cousin, and not a rat.'

The little field-vole looked at the water-vole and knew at once that he had nothing to fear. His cousin was a big, stumpy fellow, with thick reddish-brown fur in which a few greyish hairs grew. His muzzle was rounded and his tail was much shorter than a rat's.

'Yes, I see you are not a rat,' said the little vole, thankfully. 'Sometimes *I* am mistaken for a mouse.'

'You know,' said the water-vole, pulling a long face, 'it is a dreadful thing to be mistaken for a *rat* – far worse than being thought a mouse. Humans often kill me, thinking I am a water-rat, though I am nothing of the kind. *I* couldn't eat the things a rat eats! I am a harmless little fellow, and I like to eat grass and waterweed. It is very hard to be like a rat.'

The field-vole felt sorry for his big cousin.

'Do you always live by the water?' he asked.

'Oh yes,' said the water-vole. 'I love the water. I will show you how well I can swim in a minute. My home is in a burrow here, and it has an entrance below the water and an entrance in the bank here, too. At night I come out to feed. I do not usually look for food in the daytime, but this morning was so fine and warm that I could not help coming out to bask in the sunshine. Can I offer you a nice tasty bit of willow shoot?'

'Well, I do feel hungry,' said the small field-vole.

'Come along, then, to my dining-table,' said the water-vole. He led the way to the reeds that grew thickly by the side of the pond. In one place he had nibbled off the stems or flattened them, making a kind of platform. This was his dining-table. It was littered with the remains of other meals. The big vole offered the field-vole a tender shoot of willow and a piece of horsetail stem.

'Do you build your nest on this platform?' asked the little vole, looking round.

'I did last year,' said the water-vole, chewing a willow shoot. 'I and my wife made a round nest of reeds and grasses here, and brought up our young ones quite safely. The year before that we built our nest underground, but a flood came and swamped our nursery. Where do *you* build, cousin?'

'Oh, not underground,' said the little vole.

'My wife builds a grassy nest somewhere along-side one of our runs above ground. I store food underground for the cold days. I should like you to come and have a meal with me, if you will. I have acorns, beech-mast and a few seeds.'

'I will come,' began the big vole – and then suddenly he stopped and looked frightened. The little vole saw him staring into the air. He looked up and saw, to his amazement, an enormous bird sailing downwards with wide-spread wings. It was a large grey heron coming down to the pond to fish.

The heron spied the two little voles on the reedy platform, and altered her course. Two tasty morsels for dinner! But the two voles did not wait! The field-vole rushed to the bank and cowered under a stone, calling in a high, squeaky voice to his big cousin to come, too.

But the water-vole took no notice. He dived straight into the pond! Plop! It was a beautiful dive. The field-vole watched his cousin swimming swiftly across the water. He swam with his hind legs and held his front paws up against his chin. The heron landed in the water and held her strong beak ready to spear the little swimmer – but just as the heron pounced downwards the water-vole dived again! Down into the water he went, and reached a hole in the bank a good way under water. He scrambled in and forced his way up the tunnel to his dry little room above. There he sat in safety, gasping in terror.

'It is a good thing I have an entrance under water!' he thought. 'I should never have escaped if I hadn't had my hole ready for me here. So the heron has come back again! I had better leave this pond for a while. I wonder if my little cousin, the field-vole, would let me share his hole until the heron is gone again.'

He waited until the sun had gone and the night had crept over the cold fields. The heron flapped his wings and went away – but the water-vole felt sure that he would come back again soon. It was a favourite pond of his in the winter-time.

The water-vole crept out of his hole by the above-ground entrance and listened hard. There was not a sound to be heard. The vole was listening for the screech of the barn owl, who loved to hunt at night for mice and voles. But the owl was hunting over another field far away. The water-vole crept through the reeds and ran towards the hedgerow. When he reached the bank there he lifted his blunt muzzle and sniffed gently. He was trying to find the smell of the field-vole. At last he smelt what he wanted, and followed his nose to the hole where the field-vole lived.

'Are you here, cousin?' he called, softly.

'Oh, is it you?' squeaked a frightened voice, and the little vole came running up to the entrance of his underground tunnel. 'I wondered if that great bird would spear you and kill you. Were you safe?'

'Oh yes,' said the water-vole. 'I swam to the

under-water entrance of my home and escaped that way. But I am afraid to live by the pond whilst the heron is there. Will you let me live with you until he has gone? Is there room?'

'Plenty!' cried the little vole, gladly. 'Come in at once, before the stoat hunts the hedgerow. I have food to offer you and a warm room underground.'

The water-vole took a last look round – and then shot into the hole so quickly that the little vole was sent head over heels down the tunnel. He said nothing, but picking himself up fled with the water-vole down the burrow.

'The stoat!' whispered the water-vole. 'He was there behind me! He pounced – but he only caught the tip of my tail. Dear me, cousin, your bank is just as dangerous as my pond! I think I shall go back tomorrow!'

All that night the two voles crouched together in fright. When the morning came the water-vole looked out and saw that the heron had not come back to the pond. He smelt stoat again and decided to go back to the water.

'Goodbye, cousin,' he said. 'I am more at home in the water, so I think I will go back. But come to me if you are in danger at any time and I will most certainly help you!'

One Dark Night

Spring was coming in and the hedgerow was beginning to show bunches of green leaves here and there. The starry stitchworts were out on the bank and in the damp ditch below the stinging-nettles threw up fresh green shoots. All the sleepers were awake now and enjoying the warm sunshine, the soft spring showers and the feathery breezes. The snails crept out of their hiding-places, first melting the hard plate they had grown as a winter door over the opening to their shells. The rain washed them clean and their shells shone like new. Everywhere there was beauty and freshness. The birds sang madly, and all day long there was a hunting in the hedgerow for good nesting-places. The oak-tree was happy because a thrush, a chaffinch and a blackbird had all chosen to build their nests in its branches, although as yet there were no leaves showing from the clusters of big and little buds.

The folk of the hedgerow were often puzzled

by a loud shouting and barking, by the galloping of hooves and the appearance over the hill beyond of a crowd of excited human creatures. At the first sounds the rabbits fled to their burrows, the toad hopped under his stone and the hedgehog rolled himself up tightly. None of them knew that a fox was being hunted; they simply feared the strange cries and unexpected noise.

A few days back a curious thing had happened. The noise had come suddenly nearer, and across the field streamed a line of horses, following a great crowd of baying hounds. They were chasing the red fox that lived in the woods not far off. He tore up to the hedgerow, slipped through it and out on the other side. The hounds squeezed through the hedge after him, but the horsemen had to go round to the old gate. The fox ran to the stream that bounded the farther field, jumped in it, and ran up the water for a good way. Then, having thus cleverly broken his trail for the hounds behind him, he slipped out of the water on the same side as he had jumped in, and made his way back to the hedgerow under cover of the tall weeds growing on a nearby bank. The hounds were puzzled to lose the fox's trail and began to sniff about the bank of the stream, some of them jumping in. The fox dragged himself to the hedgerow, his breath coming in great gasps, for he had run a great many miles. He had hurt his leg on some barbed wire and it pained him.

He sat down and licked it, but the noise of the hounds frightened him again. He must find a safe hiding-place. He looked up and down the hedge-bank, and found a large hole leading to a rabbit's burrow. Limping painfully he went up to it, and, knowing well that he could not run any farther, squeezed himself into the hole and made his way in as far as he could.

The rabbits were terrified. 'Fox! Fox!' went the word along the burrows. But they need not have minded, for the red fox was too tired and too weak to do anything to harm them. He listened for the hounds – but they had lost the trail and wandered off in another direction, having found the scent of another fox that had passed that way the night before. The hidden fox was safe for the moment.

He lay in hiding for a few days. His leg swelled up and he could not use it. He dragged himself out of the hole to drink water from the pond, and he snapped up a small bird that had fallen from its nest in the hedge. He was in pain and he was anxious about his mate, the vixen who lived with him in his earth on the other side of the wood.

One dark night the fox crept out of the burrow and sniffed to windward. A strange smell came to him. He puzzled his head as to what it could be. It was not hare, nor rabbit; not stoat, nor weasel; it was . . . it was badger!

The fox gave a soft bark and the badger answered him with a grunt. They had met before, these two night-prowlers. The badger ran up to the fox and sniffed him over. The fox could barely see him, for it was very dark, but the starlight gave enough glimmer for him to spy the striped black and white face of the big badger.

'Your mate has been howling for you,' said the badger to the fox. 'Where have you been?'

'I was hunted and hurt my leg,' said the fox. 'I have been hiding in this hole. I have not seen you for a long time, badger. Where have *you* been?'

'I have slept most of the winter,' answered the badger, scratching at a heap of leaves, hoping to find a toad underneath, for he was hungry. 'I always sleep in the cold weather, for then it is so difficult to find food.'

'It's easy if you know where the early lambs are, and where the chickens go to roost in the

farmer's shed,' said the fox. 'I never sleep in the winter. Did you make yourself a hole somewhere?'

'Yes,' said the badger. 'I scraped an enormous hole in a woodland bank. My feet are very strong and my claws can cut through the roots of bushes and trees easily, if I come across them in my digging. I made a very deep hole, far beneath the surface, and I dug out three or four entrances to my winter home in case I should be caught by an enemy!'

'*I* shouldn't like to go to sleep in a hole that

had three or four passages to it!' said the fox.
'That seems stupid to me.'

'Well, I blocked up all the entrances before
I went to sleep there with my family, of course,'
said the badger. 'I am not so stupid as to forget
to do that! We were very cosy indeed, I can
tell you! Even during that very cold spell, when
thick ice covered all the ponds, we were warm
and comfortable. I piled great heaps of moss
and leaves into my winter home and we slept
softly on those. But now that we are awake
again, I have been cleaning out my hole. You
should see the great pile of stuff that I have
dragged outside! I hate dirty bedding. I am a
clean creature – not like you, fox, for you
always smell unpleasant to me!'

'If you leave great piles of your winter bedding outside your hole every one will know
where you live and you will be hunted, as I
have been,' said the fox.

'No, the badgers are not hunted like you,'
said the badger quietly. 'We do not kill lambs
and chickens as you do, fox. We dare not
meddle with the human creatures and their
belongings.'

'Will you tell my mate that I will return to
her tomorrow night?' asked the fox. 'I must
not leave this hiding-place until I can run fast

again, in case I meet with a dog who will chase me.'

'I will tell her if you will do something for me,' said the badger. 'Tell me where I can find a rabbit's nest. I love rooting up a nest of young rabbits. They make a fine dinner.'

'I think there is one under that clump of bracken over there,' said the fox. The badger went off, licking his lips. He was a clumsy, lumbering creature, but he made no sound as he went. He smelt under the bracken and then began to dig a hole with his claws. They were so sharp and so strong that in a moment or two he had dug a deep hole – but there was no sign of a nest there, although his sharp nose could smell the scent of young rabbits.

He went back to the fox.

'There are no rabbits there,' he said.

'There were yesterday,' said the fox. 'I saw the mother go to them.'

'She has taken them away!' cried a small, sharp voice, and a little weasel looked through a hole in the hedgerow. 'She was afraid because you were here, fox, so when you slept in your hole she took each of her rabbits and has hidden them in the big burrow on the other side of the hedge. I know, because I met her carrying one, and I ate it.'

'Interfering little creature,' muttered the fox, angrily, as the weasel ran snickering along the other side of the hedge. There was no love lost between the two, for very often they hunted along the same ground and stole each other's prey.

'You deceived me,' said the badger to the fox. 'You must have known the rabbit had taken away her young ones. You are sly and cunning, fox, and there is no truth in you. I shall not go to tell your mate you are hiding here safely. I shall tell her that you are dead in a trap, and she must go to seek another fox to live with.'

'If you do that,' said the fox, his bright eyes glinting fiercely, 'I will find my mate to-morrow, and we shall make our nest in the upper passages of your home. You do not like our smell, and you will be forced to leave your comfortable hole and make a fresh one. Your family will not like that.'

The badger snorted angrily. It was true that he could not bear the musky smell of the fox. He was a very cleanly animal, and he considered the fox a dirty and unpleasant companion, no matter how beautiful his red coat was, or how magnificent his fine brush-tail! He remembered clearly that two winters ago he and his family had all had to leave their comfortable home deep in the earth because two foxes had made their home in one of the tunnels leading to his big hidden chamber. After the badger family had gone the foxes had taken possession of the cosy hole, so well lined with moss and leaves, and had brought up a family of six little cubs there. The badger remembered this, and snapped angrily at the fox, who at once retreated into the hole behind him. He feared the badger's strong, interlocking teeth.

'I will tell your mate what you say,' growled the badger at last. 'But you must promise me not to come near my home, for we badgers are clean and cannot live with you foxes.'

'I promise,' said the fox, yawning. What did he care where he and his mate lived? There were plenty of holes to take from the rabbits! They need go to no trouble for themselves. If the rabbits objected, then they would be eaten!

The badger went lumbering off, grunting. His striped face shone strangely in the darkness. The fox lay comfortably in his hole. Tomorrow his leg would be healed. He could go back to his mate. Together they would go to the farmer's fowl-run and force their way into the shed. Then they would have a wonder-

71

ful feast. The fox shut his eyes and dreamed happily.

The next day he was gone, and the hedgerow came alive again. Rabbits hopped about freely, happy that their enemy was gone. The hare ran up once or twice. The mice chattered in squeaky voices, and the birds were glad that there was now no enemy beneath the hedge, waiting to snatch up their helpless young ones when they fell. And soon every one forgot the fox and no longer feared him.

Only the badger was angry – the fox and his mate had broken their promise after all, and had made their home in one of the tunnels leading to his dwelling-place. The badger could not bear their smell, and soon, with angry grunts and growls, he was busy pushing his family out into the moonlight. They must find another home!

Brer Frog and
Brer Toad

The month of March was kind to the hedgerow
folk. East winds blew, but only gently, and at
midday the sun shone down so warmly that the
primroses came out by the dozen on the bank
under the oak-tree. They shone there, pale and
yellow, in their rosettes of green leaves. Some
early purple violets flowered too, for they were
sheltered by the hedge, and as little mice ran
to and fro they smelt the hidden blossoms in
surprise, wondering what the fragrance was.

The ivy was still thick and green, but the
other parts of the hedge were bare, though
swelling with rosy hawthorn buds. Only the
strands of honeysuckle had leaves, green and
tender; but the honeysuckle was always early.
Soon the hedge would be green again, for the
warm March sun was coaxing all the leaf-buds
to sprout.

The creatures of the hedgerow were full of

excitement and delight. After the long winter it was glorious to feel the warm fingers of the sun reaching down into hole and burrow. The rabbits leapt about madly. The hedgehog woke up and came out one night, hungry and thirsty, looking for something to eat. The dormouse woke too, quite a different-looking creature from the one that had fallen asleep in the autumn – for now he was thin and flabby.

Under a big stone on the bank was a toad. It was a good hiding-place, moist and sheltered. The toad had used it for his home for many years, for he was an old fellow, wise and cunning. He had scraped out a small hollow with his back legs, and his body fitted into the hole very well. The big stone jutted out over him, and there he lived, snug and safe. All the hedgerow folk knew him, and only the very young mice feared him – for he had been known to make his dinner off small mice once and again, when he needed a change from beetles and slugs.

The stoat had often sniffed under the big stone as he ran silently by. He could smell toad there. But he did not try to hunt the toad out. He had been warned against toads by all the older stoats, so he left the big toad alone. The stoat thought that the toad lived a dull life, for

all the winter through, night or day, the toad never left his stone. There he squatted by himself, unmoving.

But he was not dull. He was asleep. There were no insects about in the winter-time, and he did not like the cold. So he slept deeply, not feeling the cold frost, nor missing his food. No one looking under the stone would see him, for he was as brown as the earth and as still as the stone itself.

But now that March had come, and the air grew warm, the old toad stirred himself. He opened his eyes with difficulty, for his long

sleep had stuck the lids together. He rubbed
them with one of his front feet, and soon he
could see. He sat still for a few minutes,
remembering. This was his stone. Outside was
the hedgerow. Slugs were to be found in the
ditch. Beetles ran on the bank. He was hungry
– very hungry.

Then he felt something else too – something
stronger than hunger. He wanted to get to some
water. He wanted to croak loudly. He wanted
to find a toad-wife, and ask her to lay some
eggs for him.

A noise came to his ears. It was the croaking
of frogs in the pond nearby! They had awakened too, and had come up from the mud at
the bottom, excited by the spring sunshine.
The toad felt more and more excited. His
throat swelled and he gave a hoarse and gurg-
ling croak.

'Oh, so you are awake at last,' said a voice,
and a brilliant eye looked under the stone. It
belonged to a frog, a large one who had slept
the winter through at the bottom of the muddy
ditch, with his head in a watery hole. He had
awakened the day before, and had remembered
the toad under the stone. They had often
croaked to one another the year before.

'Yes, I'm awake,' said the toad, blinking his

beautiful coppery eyes. 'Is the weather very warm?'

'Yes, very,' said the frog, delightedly. 'It is the warmest spring we have had for a long time. There are hundreds of frogs in the pond already. I came to see if you were awake yesterday, but you weren't. Are you coming to the pond?'

'Of course,' said the toad, trying to move his legs, which were stiff after his long sleep. 'Wait for me. My legs are like wood, but they will soon feel right again.'

The frog sat outside in the sunshine, keeping a sharp look-out for any enemy. His bright eyes looked all round him, and his back legs were ready to leap at any moment. His coat was yellowish-green, and matched the grass around him very well. He heard the croaking of the frogs in the pond and he was anxious to join them. It was wonderful to be awake again, warm in the sunshine, with all the excitements of spring-time before him.

The toad stretched out a leg. Then very slowly he crawled forward from under the mossy stone. As he came to the sunshine, a little shadow passed over him. At once both the frog and the toad sat as if frozen stiff. The shadow was cast by a small fly. It came to rest on a blade of grass just in front of the frog.

From the frog's wide mouth flicked out a long tongue. Its sticky end touched the little fly, and before the insect knew what was happening the tongue was inside the frog's mouth again, and he was being swallowed. The frog's eyes shut as he swallowed the morsel, and then opened again.

'That was good,' he said. 'Very small, but quite good. Our tongues are useful, don't you think so, toad?'

The toad agreed. He too had a long tongue fixed cleverly to the front of his mouth, instead of to the back. The tip of his tongue pointed down his throat! It was easy to flick it out quickly and aim it at any fly or beetle passing near.

'Come,' said the frog, impatiently. 'We must go to the pond. We shall not find wives for ourselves unless we do.'

The toad crawled right out of his hole under the stone. For a few moments he stayed still, blinking in the glare of the sun. Then he began to move towards the water, crawling along, or making short hops. The frog took enormous leaps, and had to keep waiting for the toad.

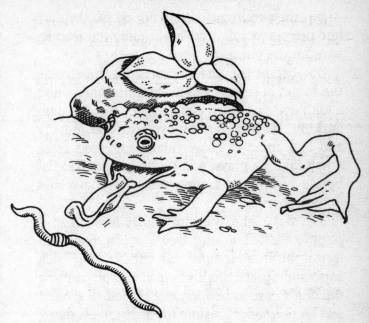

Soon they came to a puddle. In it were two frogs, croaking excitedly.

'Why don't you go to the big pond instead of wasting your time here?' asked the toad, curiously.

'We might as well lay eggs here,' said the frogs in a croaking chorus. 'Why not?'

'You are foolish,' said the toad. 'Tomorrow this puddle will have dried up – then your eggs will shrivel in the sun and you will have no children.'

But the two frogs took no notice. So the toad left them and followed his friend, the leaping frog, to the pond.

But before they had reached it, there came the sound of scampering feet behind them, and a loud noise sounded above them. It was a dog, barking! He had seen the two creatures moving and had come to chase them. The toad froze down into the grass, and the frog crouched flat beside him, each hoping that the dog would not see them.

The dog, who was not much more than a puppy, sniffed at the frog's moist body. In terror the frog straightened out his long back legs, and sprang high up into the air, hitting the dog's nose as he jumped. He fell to ground and leapt again, this time towards the gleaming pond. Plop! He was safely in it before the dog had recovered from his fright and astonishment.

But the toad could not leap away. He was a slow mover and could not hope to escape an enemy. He lay perfectly still, but over his back began to shine tiny drops of moisture which were oozing out from the knobby warts that covered his brown body. A nasty smell arose from the crouching toad. The dog sniffed it in disgust. This creature did not smell nice. He smelt dangerous. He put his head down to the toad and sniffed again. Then he opened his mouth and cautiously tried to pick up the toad – but as soon as he tasted the toad's back he started back in dismay. What a horrible taste! What a disgusting smell! This creature was poisonous. The dog shook his head to get rid of the taste in his mouth, and then trotted away. Never, never again would he interfere with toads or frogs!

The frog popped his head out of the pond. His big eyes looked scared. Was his friend eaten? No! He was on the bank, quite safe, just about to let himself drop into the water.

The pond was full of croaking, wriggling frogs and toads. The toad looked about for a wife, and chose a big brown toad with lovely, coppery eyes. Together they sank to the bottom of the pond to choose a place for their eggs. The frog also found a wife for himself, a lively, green-backed creature with a merry, bubbling croak.

The sun shone down all that day and the next. Rabbits came and looked in wonder at the excitement in the pond. The heron flew down, but even he could not quiet the happy creatures. He caught five frogs and then flew

away. Frog-catching was easy in the spring-
time!

'Come and look at my eggs!' croaked the
toad to the frog, one day, when he met his
friend under a water-lily leaf. The frog swam
down to the bottom of the pond with him, and
gazed in surprise at a double string of jelly
which was wound round and round and in and
out of the stems of water-plants. The little
black eggs stood out boldly in the jelly, and
the frog could see that the tadpoles would soon
hatch.

'What a long string of eggs!' he croaked. 'I
never lay my eggs in strings. Now come and
see mine!'

The toad swam to the surface of the pond
with the proud frog. He saw a great bunch of
eggs all in a mass of white jelly together. Little
black specks here and there showed where the
tadpoles were growing in the jelly.

'These eggs were laid at the bottom of the
pond,' said the frog. 'But the jelly soon swelled
up and floated to the surface so that the sunshine could warm them and hatch them. Look!
Over there is some frog-spawn that was laid
before mine. The tadpoles are hatching out
already!'

So they were. The toad saw hundreds of tiny

little tailed creatures wriggling about on the jelly mass. They had little suckers under their bodies with which they clung to the jelly.

'Soon they will grow big and in a few weeks they will have their legs,' said the frog. 'Hind legs first, and then front legs. Then their tails will disappear, and they will be little frogs, anxious to find a home for themselves in our hedgerow.'

'Toad tadpoles grow their front legs first,' said the old toad. 'It is better to grow front legs first.'

'Not at all,' said the frog. 'All well-brought-up tadpoles grow their hind legs first of all.'

'Croak, croak, croak,' began the toad, angrily, and the frog began to shout too – but suddenly there came a cry of warning: 'Ducks! Ducks!' And down to the pond flew two wild ducks, one a beautiful drake and the other his sober-brown wife. All the frogs and toads at once disappeared, and nothing more was heard about tadpoles and their ways.

'Quack!' said the drake, annoyed. 'Why do frogs always go when we come?' Why, indeed!

The Strange Egg

There were many more birds about the hedge-row in April and May than in March, for the nightingale were back again, the willow-wrens had arrived, and the chiff-chaff called his name time after time from the alder-trees. The steel-blue swallows had left the warmth of Africa and had come to the spring-time of Britain. They darted about in the blue sky, crying 'fee-tafeetit, feetafeetit' in their pretty, twittering voices.

The big grey cuckoo, with his barred chest, had come back too. He cried 'Cuckoo! Cuckoo!' all day long in the month of May. There were times when the hedgerow folk were tired of his voice, but he still went on cuckoo-ing. He tried to shout more loudly than any other cuckoo. The birds thought him strange, for he could not sing, neither could he chirrup or twitter. He spoke with a human voice.

Another thing that the birds disliked about the cuckoo was his barred chest, which reminded them of the sparrowhawk who came swooping round the hedgerow to hunt small birds. Sometimes a sparrow would spy the cuckoo sitting in the oak-tree, and, seeing the barred chest, would cry 'Chirrup! Chirrup! The hawk is in the oak-tree! Come and mob him!'

All the sparrows near by would fly up, and the chaffinches would go too. What a noise and commotion they made! They would surround the cuckoo and shout at him until he was angry and frightened. Then he would spread his sharp-pointed wings and fly away, crying 'Cuckoo!' loudly as he flew.

'*I* knew it was only a cuckoo,' the robin would say, flicking his wings over his back. 'I could have told you that before you began to mob him – but it was good fun to watch you all.'

The brown hedge-sparrow, that quiet and sober little bird, no relation of the noisy, ill-bred house-sparrows, called to the robin: 'Come and see my nest! It is finished!'

The robin went to see it. It certainly was beautiful. The hedge-sparrow had built it right in the hedgerow itself, and it was well hidden. First of all the hedge-sparrows had put a little foundation of twigs, and on these had built a neat and pretty nest of moss and grass. Inside was a soft lining of wool, taken from the hedge against which the sheep had rubbed themselves. The little hen-bird had made the nest round and cup-like by getting into it and moving herself round and round.

'You make a nice nest,' said the robin. 'Mine is good, too. You would never guess where it is!'

'Oh, somewhere peculiar!' said the hedge-sparrow, getting into her nest again, and settling down comfortably.

'It's in an old boot down in the ditch,' said the robin, with a creamy trill. 'I've two eggs there already.'

'Well, go away now,' said the hedge-sparrow, sleepily. 'I'm going to lay an egg. I'm going to sit here and look at the blue sky through the little green leaves that keep moving in the wind, and perhaps my egg will be as blue as the sky I love so much.'

In a week's time the robin visited the little hedge-sparrow again, and she proudly showed him her eggs. She had four, and they were indeed as blue as the sky. They were really beautiful.

'One of my eggs has hatched already,' said the robin. 'Tell me if you see any of those grey squirrels about, hedge-sparrow, for I am so afraid they will steal my nestlings.'

The hedge-sparrow promised, and kept a look-out for the squirrels. But for days she did not see one. Neither did her little brown mate, who sometimes took a turn at sitting on the eggs when his wife was tired and wanted to stretch her wings for a while.

But somebody else came to the hedgerow, looking for birds' nests – not the squirrel, nor the stoat; not the jay, nor the black jackdaw. It was the big grey cuckoo, a hen-bird with bright eyes. The cuckoo peered here and there in the hedge, she looked in the ditch, but she didn't see the robin's nest. No, she didn't think of looking inside a dirty old boot!

She saw the hedge-sparrow sitting on her nest in the middle of the green hedgerow. The cuckoo sat up in the oak-tree, quite silent, and watched as best she could. She heard a twitter of excitement because one of the blue eggs had just hatched out. She heard the two birds chattering in delight to one another, and then the little brown cock-bird sat up on the topmost spray of the hedge and began to sing a pretty little song to tell everyone that at last an egg had hatched out into a tiny chick.

The cuckoo made a bubbling noise in her

throat, and flew down to the ground. She sat there for a while and when she stood up she looked for the egg she had just laid. It was a surprisingly small egg for such a big bird as the cuckoo. It was a bluish colour, but not so blue as the hedge-sparrow's wonderful eggs.

The cuckoo saw the cock and hen hedge-sparrow fly out of the hedge to find food for the newly hatched youngster. This was her chance. Taking her egg in her big beak she flew to the hedgerow. She forced her way in to the hidden nest and carefully put her own egg there. Looking round, she saw the hen hedge-sparrow flying back, and she hurriedly picked up one of the bright-blue eggs and flew off with it, leaving her own egg in the nest.

She dropped the hedge-sparrow's egg on the ground. It smashed, but the cuckoo paid no heed. She had done what she wanted to do – put her egg into another bird's nest, and got rid of it. Now she wouldn't have the trouble of sitting on it, or of looking after the young one when it hatched out!

The wise old toad watched the cuckoo flying hurriedly away, and saw the yellow splash of the dropped egg in the grass. He crawled over to it and flicked out his long tongue to taste the egg. The hedgehog appeared and ran over to it too, for he dearly loved the taste of an egg.

'That's the cuckoo up to her old tricks again,' said the toad, who knew nearly everything about the hedgerow creatures, for he had lived so long.

'She's a wicked creature to give other birds the trouble of rearing her young ones,' said the hedgehog.

'Ah well, it's their own fault,' said the wise toad. 'It is said that she started her bad ways long long ago, because the other birds wouldn't let her nest. They thought she was like a hawk, you know, and pulled her nest to pieces every time she started to build – so in the end she gave it up and put her egg into some one else's nest!'

The hen hedge-sparrow had flown back to her nest by this time and had once more settled down on it. She had given the eggs a glance, and had not even noticed that one seemed a little different – not so blue and just a little bigger than the rest. She felt sure they were all her eggs.

She was very happy. Her eggs were hatching, her little mate sang to her often and brought her titbits, and the weather was sunny and warm. One by one the youngsters came out of the egg, and last of all the cuckoo's egg hatched.

The tiny cuckoo was a strange-looking creature. He was black, bare and ugly, and dear me, he was the hungriest of all! He had a loud voice, and the hen hedge-sparrow was so alarmed at his cries of hunger that she went off to find grubs as well as her mate, leaving the nest with the four babies at the bottom.

The young cuckoo felt uncomfortable. A tiny hedge-sparrow was pressing against his back and he could not bear to feel it. He fell into such a fit of rage that his whole body stiffened itself and his tiny wings stretched out. Somehow he got the other little bird into a hollow on his back and as soon as he felt him there he began to climb slowly up the edge of the nest, backwards, using his wings as hands. It was strange to see him. The blackbird, who was sitting on a branch above, was amazed, but it was not her nest, so she said nothing.

At last the cuckoo reached the top of the nest. He gave a shake and the young hedge-sparrow rolled over the edge and fell through the hedge to the ground below, cheeping piteously. The cuckoo sank back to the bottom of the nest, and lay there, quite exhausted. The hen hedge-sparrow, hearing the cheep of her young one, and fearing the grey squirrels, flew back to her nest. There was no squirrel there, so she sat down and covered the three young ones with her wings. She did not seem to hear the cheeping of the little fledgling outside the nest.

The cock-bird came back to the hedgerow and saw the little bird on the ground, quite helpless – but he took no notice of it. He did not think it could be one of his little ones. Only the robin was sad and upset. It was impossible, he knew, to carry a young one back to its nest once it had fallen out, but a robin is tender-hearted, and he was sad to hear its little chee-pings. He hopped over to it and looked at it with his head on one side – but soon he flew away quickly, crying 'Stoat! Stoat!'

The stoat too had heard the shrill cheep-cheep of the little nestling. It snapped up the tiny bird, and ran on its way again, resolving to come that way on the following morning.

Sure enough, the next day there was another little hedge-sparrow baby tipped out of the nest by the cuckoo – and on the following day the third one lay on the ground, cheeping. The stoat ate them all.

And now there was only the little cuckoo left in the nest. It was content. It lay there, fat and

happy, for it had all the food brought to the nest. The two hedge-sparrows were proud of their enormous child. They did not seem to notice that the others had gone. They sang all day about the large nestling and many birds came to look at it.

'He is so big, so strong!' sang the little birds, proudly. 'He is the biggest hedge-sparrow that ever lived! He eats like a big jay, and calls as loudly as a rook!'

The little cuckoo certainly had a harsh and piercing voice. He was always hungry and called all day long. The robins in the ditch became so tired of his voice that to silence him they too fed him, bringing him grubs and the large and hairy woolly-bear caterpillars that he loved so much.

At last the cuckoo had to leave the nest, for

he grew far too big for it! He was three times the size of the hedge-sparrows now, and when they brought him food they stood on his shoulder to give it to him! It was a strange sight to see. But the hedge-sparrows were delighted with the baby cuckoo. They thought him truly marvellous, and talked about him to every one in the hedgerow.

One day the old toad saw the cuckoo on the grass pecking at a worm. He blinked his coppery eyes and croaked deeply when the cock hedge-sparrow sang to tell him that the big bird was his nestling.

'Urrrrk, urrrrk!' said the toad, wisely. 'If that's a hedge-sparrow, friend, then you are a cuckoo!' And not another word would he say to the puzzled little hedge-sparrow!

The Bumble-Bee Hums

All the hedgerow folk liked to hear the humming of the bees. It was a summery sound, lazy and warm. The earliest bees had been out in March, seeking for the flowers that opened on the bank below. More bees had come in April, and very soon there had been heard the loud booming of the big brown and yellow bumble-bee. She *did* make a noise. Zooooooooom! Zoooooooooom! It was a lovely droning sound, never heard in the cold days of winter.

The bumble-bee had slept all through the winter in a little hole on the north side of the hedgerow-bank. It was a cold hole, full of bitterness when the north winds blew in January and February. But the bumble-bee had chosen it carefully. She knew that to choose a warm hole on the south side of the hedge would be dangerous. The sun came early to the south bank, and sent its warm beams into every nook and cranny there, waking up all the small slee-pers. But to wake up on a sunny day in Febru-ary and crawl forth might mean death when the frost returned at night. It was best to sleep in a cold place, unwarmed by the early sun-shine of the year, and not to wake until all fear of frosts was past.

The bumble-bee had carefully made a honey-pot for herself before going to sleep. Then, if by chance she should awake, she could have a sip of honey from her pot and need not run the risk of leaving her hole. The hole was small. It had been made by a worm, and the bee squat-ted down in the enlarged room at the end of the hole, her honey-pot beside her. She did not wake until February, and then although the sun was shining warmly on the south side of the hedge, her hole was still rimmed around by frost and she did not stir out. She sipped her honey and went to sleep again.

At last, on a warm spring day, she walked out, feeling rather top-heavy and a little dazed with her long cold sleep. She spread her wings and the hedgerow heard once again the loud booming hum that it liked so much in the sum-mer-time. The warm days must be coming if the bumble-bee was about!

The bee decided to look for a new hole – a

warm one this time, and a bigger one. She knew the hedgerow well, and thought it would be good to find one there, for then she would not need to learn new surroundings. So she began her hunt.

There was one rather big hole on the south side, but the bumble-bee came out quickly after one look, for a most enormous spider lived there! She looked under an old stone and saw a fat toad peering at her with gleaming eyes. He knew she was dangerous and did not flick out his tongue to eat her. She backed out quickly. Then she flew to another part of the bank, humming busily, enjoying herself in the hot sun. And at last she found exactly the right hole!

It had been made by mice, and their smell still hung about the little hole. The bumble-bee altered the hole to her liking and then fetched in some moss. She crawled out again and brought back some grass. Then she visited some flowers and returned with pollen which she packed into the hole. She looked at the heap of moss, grass and pollen, and decided it was time to lay her eggs.

So she built some egg cells and put pollen into each. Then she laid her eggs, one in each

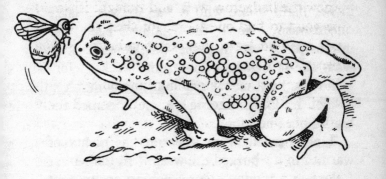

cell, white, long-shaped eggs and spread herself over them to brood them. By her were several of her honey-pots, full of honey. Soon her eggs hatched out into grubs – but how hungry they were! They ate up all the pollen in their cells, and the bumble-bee bit a tiny hole in each cell, and passed more food through to her growing children.

Now the big bumble-bee was busy all day long. She went out to find food for her first batch of children; she laid more eggs; she built more and more cells; she taught the first batch of young bees how to help her. She was happy, and the hedgerow liked to hear her going booming about her work.

One morning she heard the loud humming

of another creature near by, and she stopped in her flight to see who it was. It was a large queen-wasp, and the bumble-bee was interested to see that she was doing exactly what she herself had done some weeks before – she was hunting for a hole in the bank!

'You are late in finding a home,' boomed the big bumble-bee.

'I only awake when the sun has plenty of warmth in it,' buzzed the wasp. 'All the winter I slept in a hidden cranny behind an ivy-root in the hedge. A little mouse once woke me up when he came hunting for the nuts the squirrel hid, but he soon fled when he saw *me*!'

'*I* have a fine nest in an old mouse-hole,' hummed the bee, settling down beside the big queen-wasp. 'Come and see it.'

But the wasp was in a hurry. She was anxious to find a hole for herself and begin her building. The summer would soon be here and she must lay her eggs. She ran to a hole and crawled inside to see if it would suit her. But a big beetle was there, and showed her his great, ugly jaws. The wasp hurried out again and flew to another hole. This was too big, and full of rubbish.

At last she found exactly what she needed. This was an old tunnel made by the mole the summer before. Part of the roof had fallen in at the back. The wasp walked all over the hole, touching the walls with her feelers. This was a good place. She was pleased with it. She crawled up to the roof and found there the root of a hawthorn-bush jutting out. She could hang her nest from that.

She left the hole and flew up into the air, circling round as she did so, noticing everything round her hole – the stone near by – the tuft of grass – the thistle – all these things would help her to know her hole again. Then she flew higher still into the air, and noticed bigger things – the nearby ditch, the hedgerow itself, the big bramble-spray that waved high in the air. Ah, she would know her way back again now!

The queen-wasp was going to build a city and be its ruler. She was going to have thousands of subjects, who would work for her night and day. She was longing to begin, for the warm sun had heated her blood and given her strength.

She flew off to the common up on the hill, and looked about her as she went. She was hunting for a piece of oak from which she could take a scraping to start her city. She found a gate-post and settled down on it. She bit a piece of wood out, a mere shaving, with her strong jaws. She chewed it and chewed it until it was paper-pulp. Then back she flew to the hole she had taken for her own. She crawled in – and immediately began a fierce buzzing, for there were three ants there! She drove her sting into each one and threw them out of the hole, little curled-up brown things, poisoned by her sting.

She stuck the paper pellet to the root at the top of the hole and then went off for more. In and out she flew all day long, building the roof of her house first, for the wasp-people live in topsy-turvy homes! Every time she left the hole she carried with her a pellet of earth, for she wanted to have plenty of room for her city.

She often met the big bumble-bee, who told her that she had now plenty of workers to help her, for many of her grubs had grown into bees, and did her work.

'Come and play for a while,' said the bumble-bee. 'The fields are full of flowers.'

'I have no use for flowers,' said the wasp, impatiently. 'Leave me, cousin. I am too busy. I have many things to do, and I have as yet no helpers as you have! What there is to be done I do myself.'

Soon there was a pile of earth outside the old

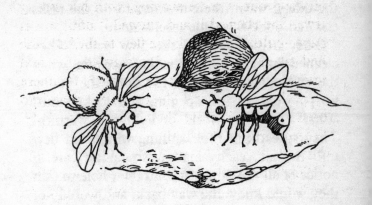

mole-hole, and inside, built safely under an umbrella-like covering of grey paper, were many wasp-cells, each containing a small grub. They hung head downwards in their cells, and were tightly glued to the top so that they could not fall out of the hole at the bottom. Soon they grew large and fat, and were so wedged in that they could not have fallen out if they had wanted to.

Then each grub spun a silk sheet over the cell-opening and formed a cocoon. The queen-wasp waited impatiently for them to come out of their cells, and at last the time came. Each little wasp bit through its cell and came out. They cleaned themselves up, and then looked round the nest. Very soon they were helping the queen-wasp, their mother, to do the tasks she had done for some weeks alone.

They helped to feed the new grubs. They cleaned the nest – and then one morning, when the sun came right into the hole, the young wasps went to the opening and looked out. What a glorious world of light and warmth! They spread out their shining wings and flew into the air, each small wasp taking careful notice of all the things around their hole so that they would know the way back, and would not get lost. Then off they went, all knowing exactly what to do, although they had never done their new tasks before.

Some of them found the old oak post from which their mother had scraped shavings to make the paper-pulp she used in building her city. They too took scrapings and chewed them into pulp, taking the pellets home again to build on to their nest, which was now three stories high. Other wasps went to a sunny wall on which many flies crawled. They caught the flies, cut off their wings, heads and legs, and carried them back to the nest to feed the young grubs. One wasp found a hiding-place in which four moths crouched, and, cutting off their wings, carried the bodies away for food. They were all busy.

They had their enemies, and so had the young bumble-bees, who were also helping their mother in the nest. The spotted fly-catcher had come back from its winter haunts and darted at the passing bees and wasps, as well as at the flies. Even the queen-wasp herself had a narrow escape one day. The great tit would sometimes wait outside the hole where the bumble-bee had her nest and would pounce on an unwary bee just leaving.

One day all the bees and the wasps heard a strange noise. It was a high humming, very shrill and loud, like a wasp or bee army on the march. Every wasp and every bumble-bee flew to see what it was – and they saw a strange sight! A great cloud of honey-bees was coming over the field towards the hedgerow. It was led by the queen-bee, and thousands of bees were following her. The queen-wasp flew near and demanded to know what had happened, for she was excited and half-frightened by the tremendous humming.

'We come from a hive far away,' boomed the queen-honey-bee. 'I had so many worker bees that the hive became too small. So I have brought half the hive away with me and I am looking for a new home. I have left behind me some princesses in the hive. One of them will become queen in my place.'

'*We* do not swarm!' said the queen-wasp. 'I make my city as big as I want it.'

'You are only a wasp!' buzzed the honey-bee. 'Your city will crumble to nothing in the autumn, all your people will die! But my people live with me, for we store up honey for the cold days!'

The wasp shivered. She thought of the days to come when the frost would creep on her again – when her people would freeze and die – her beautiful city be eaten by hungry mice! But what did she care? *She* would live! Next spring she would come again and once more build a marvellous city. She buzzed happily and flew off to her hole. The swarm settled on the lowest branch of the oak-tree, and then in a short while flew off again, no one knew where.

'Zooooooom!' buzzed the bumble-bee to the queen-wasp. 'Who would be a hive-bee and live in slavery? Not I! Give me a hole in a bank and let me be my own mistress! Zooooooom!'

Wicked Rat

The hedgerow was quiet in the hot afternoon sun of July. The far-away hills were very blue, and the few clouds in the sky were silver-white. The pond was as blue as the sky and not even a little black moor-hen chick was to be seen making ripples on the surface. It was too hot to sing – too hot to chirrup – too hot to stir from the shelter of the hedgerow! The big oak-tree stood quite still, and not even a leaf moved, for there was no breeze anywhere.

The cuckoo no longer called from the woods. Even the small yellowhammer who loved to sing about his little bit of bread and *no* cheese, sitting on the telegraph wires by the oak-tree, was too hot to open his beak. Everything was drowsy, half-asleep in the hot sun, peaceful and contented.

But no – some one was astir after all! Some one came running down the ditch; a long grey-brown form with a sharp muzzle, big ears and long tail. It was the wicked rat, hungry and fierce.

The hedgerow folk had almost forgotten the rat during the winter. He had lived about the farm then, picking up a good living in the corn-stacks. He had found the farmer's buried mangolds and had gnawed hundreds of them. But when the warm days came he had left the farm and gone out into the fields. For one thing the farmer's three kittens had now grown into big, sharp-clawed cats, and the rat was afraid of them. For another thing the farmer was sensible and had killed no weasels, for he knew that weasels like a meal of rats. So three weasels had come hunting about the farm-yard and the rat had run away. He was very much afraid of the fierce little creatures.

He had gone to the hedgerow. There he had made his runs, and had burrowed under the hedge in one place. He had made runs in the soft earth by the pond, too, and there were many holes there that mice and lizards would not go near because they knew that the wicked rat might come out at any moment.

The rat was cruel. He was fierce, brave, clever. Not one of the hedgerow folk could get the better of him, not even the stoat who sometimes came along the ditch to see what he could find. Once a weasel came too, but the rat smelt him a good way off and long before the weasel came into sight the rat had disappeared.

The hedgerow folk grumbled bitterly to the little field mice, for they were the small cousins of the rat.

'Why do you not tell him to go away? He is a hateful creature. He has no kindness in him, not even to his own family.'

'That is true,' said the long-tailed field mouse. 'I know that he eats his own children sometimes, and if he finds a rat that is ill or hurt, he will eat him too. He is wicked. Even the humans hate him, for they say he brings illness to them. But what can *I* do? He might eat me if I asked him to go away!'

The hedgerow folk went on grumbling, but nobody dared to do anything. The rat lived unmolested in the hedgerow, and had already brought up two families there, watched over by his fierce wife. Now there were nineteen rats about the hedgerow and nothing and nobody was safe.

The robin's second eggs had all been eaten by the rats. Three young birds belonging to the freckled thrush had been eaten, and two of the little moor-hen chicks had gone the same way. The moor-hen was very angry about it and cried 'Fulluck, fulluck!' about a hundred times when she saw what the rat was doing. But she could not stop him. After that she made her chicks keep close to her by night and day.

The rabbits complained that many of their young ones had been killed, and one mother-rabbit was wild with grief when she found that the rat had discovered her hidden burrow and had eaten all her pretty youngsters so cosily nestled there.

The rat cared for nobody. He was not a friendly animal. He thought of only one thing, and that was where to get his next meal.

On this hot July afternoon the little field mouse was sitting, half-asleep, at the entrance to his burrow. It was in the warm bank. Far below, close-hidden at the end of the burrow, was his tiny mate, curled up in a nest of dry grass with her new family of youngsters, five pretty little mice like herself. She was very happy. The year before she had built her nest under a big tuft of grass in the hedge, but she had been afraid to bring up her young ones above ground whilst the rats were about. So this summer she had made an underground nursery for them.

'This burrow would be a good place to rest in for the winter,' she thought to herself, sleepily. 'We could store hips and haws here, and some acorns too. I remember last autumn that there were plenty of red hips in the hedgerow above. I climbed up into the branches and picked some, and nibbled out the seeds inside. I took an old nest belonging to the hedge-sparrow for my dining-table.'

Suddenly the little long-tailed mouse pricked up her small ears. She could hear her mate squeaking at the entrance to the burrow.

He was being very brave indeed – for he was talking to the wicked rat. The rat had come running silently along the ditch, making his way unseen beneath the tall grasses and green nettles. He had leapt up on to the bank and had suddenly seen the little field mouse.

The mouse stiffened, and then bravely called out to the rat:

'Cousin rat! You have done much harm to the folk of the hedgerow. You have killed and eaten us! Your large family is bringing fear and terror to all the little creatures that live around. Go back to the farm and return here no more.'

The fierce rat stopped in surprise. He was hungry. His nose moved as he sniffed the smell of mouse.

'Have you a family?' he asked.

'Never mind whether I have a family or not,' said the small mouse, in alarm, thinking of his tiny wife and tinier youngsters. 'Hear what I say, cousin, or we hedgerow folk will tell the weasel of you and you will be hunted even as you hunt us!'

The rat did not listen. He could smell the little mice down in the burrow, and his whiskers quivered with delight. He suddenly made a spring at the small mouse, who, squeaking with terror, tore down his hole.

Then the hot, peaceful afternoon was filled with the pitiful squealings and squeakings of the mouse family. The rat forced his way into the burrow and went straight to where the mouse was curled up about her family. He snatched at them with his sharp teeth, and before many seconds had passed each of the baby mice was gone. The mother squealed in anger and actually flung herself on the rat, biting him on the neck. But he easily shook her off, nipped her behind the ears and then ate her too.

When the other mouse saw this he fled down another tunnel, wailing as if his small heart would break. All who heard him made way for him and then ran themselves, for they knew that some great disaster had happened.

The rat was happy. He sniffed around the hole for a few seconds and then went out again. He found a tuft of grass and lay under it for a little while, enjoying the hot sun. He was satisfied.

The little field mouse was bitterly unhappy. He was full of hatred for the false and treacherous rat; he missed his pretty little wife and longed for his small youngsters. He touched no food that day, and when night came he went to cool himself under a big stone on the bank. There he found the toad, also cooling himself.

'The wicked rat has taken my little mate and my small mice,' said the mouse, fluttering his nose as he remembered.

'It is time that the rat went away,' said the toad, slowly. 'He is the enemy of the whole world.'

'You are wise,' said the long-tailed mouse, looking at the toad with sad little eyes. 'Tell me how to get rid of the wicked rat. Who will do that for us? The stoat cannot catch him and if the weasel comes, he knows, and disappears.'

'I remember once before,' said the old toad, blinking his round eyes, 'I remember once before that rats came to this hedgerow and brought death and grief with them. And I remember who destroyed them.'

'Who?' asked the little mouse, eagerly. 'Tell me!'

'It was the brown owl,' said the toad, remembering. 'Yes, he came night after night and watched silently for the rats. And one by one they went.'

'Let us send to the brown owl,' said the mouse. 'He lives in the woods, for I have sometimes heard him hooting. We will send the blackbird tomorrow.'

The blackbird was glad to go to find the brown owl, for the rat had tried to kill one of her nestlings in June. She flew to the woods and hunted for the brown owl. The noisy jays told her that the owl was hiding in a pine-tree, close up to the trunk, his eyes half-closed. There the blackbird found him and told him of the rats.

'I will come,' said the wise owl, opening his great eyes. 'Tonight I will come. I have a wife and five hungry youngsters, and I shall be glad of food to take to them.'

That night the hedgerow folk heard the brown owl hooting. 'Ooooooooooo!' he called. 'Oo-oo-oo-*ooo*!' It was a beautiful sound through the dark night, but all the little mice shivered, for they were as much afraid of the owl as were the rats. They kept close inside their holes – but the rats were out hunting.

The brown owl flew on wide-spread wings to the hedgerow. He flew silently, so silently that no one heard him except the little field-mouse who was listening anxiously in his hole down in the bank.

The owl flew right over the hedgerow. He looked down with his great eyes. There was no moon and the stars gave only the very faintest of light – but quite enough for the owl to see by. He was watching for the tiniest movement of the grasses which would show him where a rat ran.

And soon he saw what he was looking for! The grass moved a little – and at the same moment the owl dropped like a stone, feet foremost. His talons closed over a struggling body – it was the rat!

It was useless for the wicked rat to try to escape. He was caught in a trap – for the owl's feet closed like a vice. The brown owl flew off with the rat and gave him to his hungry mate. Then back he came again to the hedgerow – and before the night was gone seven rats were caught and taken to the nest in the old hollow tree.

The rest of the rats fled in terror far from the hedgerow. 'Brown owl!' they squealed to one another. 'Brown owl!'

And once again the small hedgerow folk lived in peace. The long-tailed mouse found another wife and had a second family – and when they wanted to run out of the burrow too soon he would say 'Come back! The wicked rat will get you! Aha! The wicked rat!'

Other great reads ⌔ *from* **Red Fox**

Further Red Fox titles that you might enjoy reading are listed on the following pages. They are available in bookshops or they can be ordered directly from us.

If you would like to order books, please send this form and the money due to:

ARROW BOOKS, BOOKSERVICE BY POST, PO BOX 29, DOUGLAS, ISLE OF MAN, BRITISH ISLES. Please enclose a cheque or postal order made out to Arrow Books Ltd for the amount due, plus 22p per book for postage and packing, both for orders within the UK and for overseas orders.

NAME _____

ADDRESS _____

_____

Please print clearly.

Whilst every effort is made to keep prices low, it is sometimes necessary to increase cover prices at short notice. If you are ordering books by post, to save delay it is advisable to phone to confirm the correct price. The number to ring is THE SALES DEPARTMENT 071 (if outside London) 973 9700.

Other great reads *from* **Red Fox**

Two books from Enid Blyton

THE BIRTHDAY KITTEN *and*
THE BOY WHO WANTED A DOG—2 books in 1!

The Birthday Kitten

Terry and Tessie, the twins, want a pet of their own very badly.
While they are playing with Terry's new boat, they notice a
small, wriggling bundle in the pond. It is a tiny, half-drowned
kitten. But what will their mother say when they take it home?

The Boy who Wanted a Dog

Donald's parents won't let him have a dog, but he's allowed
to help out at the local vet's kennels—until his father bans him
for neglecting his homework.

Sadly, Donald goes down to the kennels for one last time . . .
and what a good thing it is that he does!

ISBN 0 09 977930 7   £1.99

THE GOBLIN AEROPLANE AND OTHER
STORIES

'The strange aeroplane flew swiftly towards them, flapping its
odd red and yellow wings . . .'

It is such a nice day that Jill and Robert are doing their spelling
lessons out of doors. Before they know what is happening they
are whisked away in a goblin aeroplane into a strange adventure.

This book brings together a delightful and varied collection
of magical stories which will provide hours of entertainment.

ISBN 0 09 973590 3   £1.99

Other great reads from **Red Fox**

Adventure Stories from Enid Blyton

THE ADVENTUROUS FOUR

A trip in a Scottish fishing boat turns into the adventure of a lifetime for Mary and Jill, their brother Tom and their friend Andy, when they are wrecked off a deserted island and stumble across an amazing secret. A thrilling adventure for readers from eight to twelve.

ISBN 0 09 9477009 £2.50

THE ADVENTUROUS FOUR AGAIN

'I don't expect we'll have any adventures *this* time,' says Tom, as he and sisters Mary and Jill arrive for another holiday. But Tom couldn't be more mistaken, for when the children sail along the coast to explore the Cliff of Birds with Andy the fisher boy, they discover much more than they bargained for . . .

ISBN 0 09 9477106 £2.50

COME TO THE CIRCUS

When Fenella's Aunt Jane decides to get married and live in Canada, Fenella is rather upset. And when she finds out that she is to be packed off to live with her aunt and uncle at Mr Crack's circus, she is horrified. How will she ever feel at home there when she is so scared of animals?

ISBN 0 09 937590 7 £1.75

Other great reads ~ *from* **Red Fox**

School stories from Enid Blyton

THE NAUGHTIEST GIRL IN THE SCHOOL

'Mummy, if you send me away to school, I shall be so naughty there, they'll have to send me back home again,' said Elizabeth. And when her parents won't be budged, Elizabeth sets out to do just that—she stirs up trouble all around her and gets the name of the bold bad schoolgirl. She's sure she's longing to go home—but to her surprise there are some things she hadn't reckoned with. Like making friends . . .

ISBN 0 09 945500 5 £1.99

THE NAUGHTIEST GIRL IS A MONITOR

'Oh dear, I wish I wasn't a monitor! I wish I could go to a monitor for help! I can't even think what I ought to do!'

When Elizabeth Allen is chosen to be a monitor in her third term at Whyteleafe School, she tries to do her best. But somehow things go wrong and soon she is in just as much trouble as she was in her first term, when she was the naughtiest girl in the school!

ISBN 0 09 945490 4 £1.99

Other great reads from **Red Fox**

Two Enid Blyton books in one!

MR TWIDDLE STORIES

Mr Twiddle is a silly but lovable old man. He's always losing things—like his hat and his specs—he has trouble with a cat, gets bitten by a goose and, no matter how he tries, he just can't remember anything! This collection contains two complete books in one!

ISBN 0 09 965560 8 £1.99

MR PINKWHISTLE STORIES

Mr Pinkwhistle is small and round with pointed ears and bright green eyes. And he can do all sorts of magic . . . This collection gives you two complete books about Mr Pinkwhistle in one!

ISBN 0 09 954200 5 £1.99

MR MEDDLE STORIES

Mr Meddle is a naughty little pixie who simply *can't* mind his own business. He always tries to help others but by the time he's fed birdseed to the goldfish, sat in the butter, gone to bed in the wrong house and chased a policeman, people usually wish they'd never set eyes on him. This collection of stories gives you two complete books about Mr Meddle in one!

ISBN 0 09 965550 0 £1.99

Other great reads ← *from* **Red Fox**

Discover the exciting and hilarious books of Hazel Townson!

THE MOVING STATUE

One windy day in the middle of his paper round, Jason Riddle is blown against the town's war memorial statue.

But the statue moves its foot! Can this be true?

ISBN 0 09 973370 6 £1.99

ONE GREEN BOTTLE

Tim Evans has invented a fantasic new board game called REDUNDO. But after he leaves it at his local toy shop it disappears! Could Mr Snyder, the wily toy shop owner have stolen the game to develop it for himself? Tim and his friend Doggo decide to take drastic action and with the help of a mysterious green bottle, plan a Reign of Terror.

ISBN 0 09 956810 1 £1.50

THE SPECKLED PANIC

When Kip buys Venger's Speckled Truthpaste instead of toothpaste, funny things start happening. But they get out of control when the headmaster eats some by mistake. What terrible truths will he tell the parents on speech day?

ISBN 0 09 935490 X £1.75

THE CHOKING PERIL

In this sequel to *The Speckled Panic*, Herbie, Kip and Arthur Venger the inventor attempt to reform Grumpton's litterbugs.

ISBN 0 09 950530 4 £1.25

Other great reads from **Red Fox**

Discover the exciting Lenny and Jake adventure series by Hazel Townson!

Lenny Hargreaves wants to be a magician some day, so he's always practising magic tricks. He takes this very seriously, but his friend Jake Allen tends to scoff because he knows the tricks will probably go wrong. All the same, Lenny usually manages to round off one of the exciting and amazing adventures that they keep getting involved in with a trick that solves the problem.

The books in the series are:

The Great Ice Cream Crime
ISBN 0 09 976000 2
£1.99

The Siege of Cobb Street School
ISBN 0 09 975980 2
£1.99

The Vanishing Gran
ISBN 0 09 935480 2
£1.50

Haunted Ivy
ISBN 09 941320 5
£1.99

The Crimson Crescent
ISBN 09 952110 5
£1.50

The Staggering Snowman
ISBN 0 9956820 9
£1.50

Fireworks Galore
ISBN 09 965540 3
£1.99

And the latest story—

Walnut Whirl
Lenny and Jake are being followed by a stranger. Is he a spy trying to recover the microfilm in the walnut shell Lenny has discovered in his pocket? The chase overtakes a school outing to an Elizabethan mansion and there are many hilarious adventures before the truth is finally revealed.

ISBN 0 09 973380 3   £1.99

Other great reads from **Red Fox**

Discover the wide range of exciting activity books from Red Fox

THE PAINT AND PRINT FUN BOOK
Steve and Megumi Biddle

Would you like to make a glittering bird? A colourful tiger? A stained-glass window? Or an old treasure map? Well, all you need are ordinary materials like vegetables, tinfoil, paper doilies, even your own fingers to make all kinds of amazing things—without too much mess.

Follow Steve and Megumi's step-by-step instructions and clear diagrams and you can make all kinds of professional designs—to hang on your wall or give to your friends.

ISBN 0 09 9644606 £2.50

CRAZY KITES   Peter Eldin

This book is a terrific introduction to the art of flying kites. There are lots of easy-to-assemble, different kites to make, from the basic flat kite to the Chinese dragon and the book also gives you clear instructions on launching, flying and landing. Kite flying is fun. Help yourself to a soaring good time.

ISBN 0 09 964550 5   £2.50

Other great reads from Red Fox

CRAZY PRESENTS Juliet Bawden

Would you like to make: Pebble paper weights? Green tomato
chutney? Scented hand cream? Patchwork clowns? Leather ties?

By following the step-by-step instructions in this book you
can make a huge variety of gifts—from rattles for the very young
to footwarmers for the very old. Some cost a few pence, others
a little more but all are extra special presents.

ISBN 0 09 967080 1   £2.50

CRAZY PAPER Eric Kenneway

Origami—the Japanese art of paper folding—is easy and fun to
do. You can make boats that float, wriggling snakes, tumbling
acrobats, jumping frogs and many more fantastic creatures.

There are easy to follow instructions and clear diagrams in
this classic guide used by Japanese schoolchildren.

ISBN 0 09 951380 3   £1.95

*Other great reads from **Red Fox***

CRAZY PAINTING   Juliet Bawden

There are loads of imaginative ideas and suggstions in this easy-
to-follow activity book all about painting. First it teaches you
the basics: how to make your own vegetable dyes, mix paints,
create a fabulous marbled effect and decorate ceramics. Then
the fun begins. You can design your own curtains, make zany
brooches for your friends, create your own colourful wrapping
paper and amaze your family with hours of painting pleasure.

ISBN 0 09 954320 6   £2.25

DRESSING UP FUN   Terry Burrows

Dressing up is always fun—for a party, a play or just for a laugh!
In Dressing Up Fun you'll find loads of ideas for all kinds of
costumes and make-up. So whether you'd like to be a cowboy,
punk or witch, superman, a princess or the Empire State
Building, youll find them all in this book.

ISBN 0 09 965110 6   £2.99